Not

My

Type

Taylor Love

Taylor Made Day Dreams

Bringing an "imaginative break" to your day!

Not My Type
Copyright © 2018 Taylor Love

This is a work of fiction. Names, characters, places and incidents are either the product of the author's imagination or are used fictitiously, and any resemblance to actual persons, living or dead, business establishments, events or locales is entirely coincidental.

To the extent that the image or images on the cover of this book depict a person or persons, such person or persons are merely models. This book is for adult readership and may contain adult situations, language and sexual content.

ISBN 978-1-948383-05-9

Taylor Made Daydreams
P.O Box 85458
Westland, MI 48185
www.TaylorMadeDaydreams.com

Dedication

I dedicate my second novel to myself, for continuing my dream of writing and sharing my work. I also dedicate this book to all other new writers! Getting the characters that live in our heads *out* is no easy task. However, it's just the beginning of a complicated process of publishing and selling. Kudos to new authors who put in the many hours of writing, researching, reviewing and stressing. As they hope there are at least a *few* people out in the world, who will enjoy the hard work and creativity they put forth.

Prologue

Snuggling into the warmth at her back Mika fought not to wake up. When squeezing her eyes didn't work, she slowly let her mind come awake. She was so *not* a morning person. She felt good, relaxed, and her body had that low-key hum that only great sex gave her. Speaking of sex...something big and hard was pressed against her bottom. She gave a satisfied smile in her semi-sleep state for about three seconds before her eyes popped open.

Wait just a damn minute! She hadn't had sex in almost five months. So who in the hell nice-sized penis was rubbing up against her? Where *was* she? Mika held as still as a stone, hoping whoever was sharing the bed wouldn't realize she had woken up. Closing her eyes again, she dug deep into her memory banks.

Okay what is the last thing you remember? Umm a flight? Yes! Yes, a flight! And just like that, the puzzle pieces started to click into place, playing like a slideshow in her brain. She had come to Vegas for what she thought was a spur of the moment trip, meant to cheer up her best friend. Then she had been blindsided by Andrea saying she was getting married before taking part in her wedding. That was as far as she got before the memories trailed off. Who the hell was in her bed? Were they even in *her* bed or *his*? She had been accused of being a free spirit from time to time, and Vegas *was* Vegas, but this was taking it a bit too far!

She didn't even know anyone in Vegas, besides Andrea, Cam and...oh no! She sprung up pulling the sheet to her breasts, like some self-conscious proper lady from the 1950s, glaring at her bed partner. *"You!"*

Robert who had barely missed getting chin-checked as she flung herself up, just rolled his eyes and felt his morning wood disappear. Looking at her he stated, "Let me guess...you're not a morning person?"

"*No,* I'm not a morning person," she snapped. When he continued to calmly look at her she only got more annoyed. Clearing her throat, she asked a more pertinent question. "Whose room is this?"

"Yours," Robert answered yawning.

Mika released the breath she hadn't been aware of holding. "Good. If you don't mind, I'd like you to leave."

He looked at his watch, which she could see was a TAG Heuer and shrugged those wide, dark-chocolate shoulders of his. "Actually, that works. It's almost time to head to the airport anyway."

Robert rolled out of bed and walked the few feet to his clothing before leisurely starting to dress. He could feel her eyes on his body and smirked. Even so, he didn't linger getting dressed. He had no wish to incite any further drama from her. Finished, he walked to the door shaking his head. Mika had been bold from the moment he'd spied her in the hotel restaurant, and that impression had only continued through Cam's and Andrea's wedding celebration. She sure had been wild and ready when they'd clawed their way into bed last night. It was odd to see her reserved and prim now. Definitely didn't fit *his* impression of her personality. With his hand on the doorknob he turned back to her once more.

"Are you going to sit there all morning, clutching at the covers?"

"Just get out," Mika gritted between her teeth.

"Fine. Try not to miss the flight."

"*You* try to mind your own business, and see your way out of this room."

Mika wanted to throw something at the door as it closed. Unfortunately, the asshole she'd spent the night with was right. She didn't have time to spare on tantrums, she had a plane to catch. Rising she headed straight to the bathroom, taking a shower before getting dressed. Packing was easy, yet she still gave the room a quick look-over to make sure she wasn't leaving anything behind. When she was satisfied, she took her carry-on and rolled it to the lobby to officially check out. After that she walked quickly out to the curb, joining the queue for the airport taxi's. The first person she saw was Robert, opening the door to his own ride.

Robert felt eyes drilling into his back and turned to see Mika. Letting out a sigh, he stepped towards her and said, "Want to share a ride to the airport?"

"No, I'm good."

"You sure? We're going to the same place. Seems a little childish not to share. Wait...exactly how old are you?"

Mika clenched her teeth so hard, it was a wonder she didn't crack a tooth. "A little late to be asking my age, don't you think?"

Looking her up and down he nodded. "I suppose you got me there. Okay fine I tried," he half-mumbled to himself. He met her eyes briefly before heading back to the waiting cab. He didn't look back as the car rolled away.

Mika was officially starving by the time she reached the airport and cleared security, leaving her *just* enough time to grab a sandwich from Starbucks before it was time to board. Luckily the plane was much fuller this time, and she wasn't sitting across from Robert. Closing her eyes she got comfy before attempting to rest. She needed to forget about last night's unfortunate incident. She was going to chalk it up to the mind spell being in Vegas could put people under. It had to be. She couldn't think of another reason she would have let that *arrogant* and *annoying* man touch her. On the heel of that thought, she had a flash of memory. His knee parting her thighs, his serious mouth pulling strongly at her breast. So strongly she'd had to arch up to meet him, her hand clutching at his strong back.

"Damn it!" Startling in her seat Mika snapped her eyes open, hands clenching the armrests.

Her seatmate, a woman around sixty patted her hand in sympathy. "Don't worry honey, we'll be okay. Though I admit I don't like to fly either."

Mika gave her a distracted smile before turning to look out the window. "I've never been afraid to fly...it's the crashing that has always worried me."

Chapter One

Robert found himself wrapping up his last email of the day before straightening up his office for the weekend. He hated coming back on a Monday to an unorganized desk. It was Friday in early September, and Cam had reached out saying he had time to meet. Robert was looking forward to seeing his newly married friend in person. True they'd caught up briefly by phone when Cam had gotten back last week from his honeymoon, but it would be good to connect for real.

He made it to their meeting spot before Cam which wasn't unusual. Ordering a couple of beers for them, as he thought about how his friendship was about to change. He knew for a certainty that it would. Marriage changed a man. Made his main purpose in life to keep his home in order, and his wife happy and protected. It had been that way since the dawn of time. He was happy for Cam. The brother had always held the example of his parents' marriage as his own blueprint. And now he'd found his life partner in Andrea.

Robert's father on the other hand, had been a no good bum. A man who had left his own wife when his little boy was five, and his baby girl had barely been born. After that, Robert had only seen the man a handful of times throughout his life. When he died Robert was fifteen, and neither he nor his sister had blinked at the news. Their mother had felt it though. Robert had woken up in the middle of the night after the funeral to hear her crying her eyes out. That's what love did to you. Made you shed tears for a man that only gave you grief, heartache, and two kids to care for alone.

Which is why he wasn't sure he would ever join the "married club". Investing in someone that deeply, he wasn't sure the return was worth it. Look at all the emotional stress Cam had gone through before he and his bride got down the aisle. Thinking about it actually made Robert shift with discomfort. He hoped someone would shoot *him* if he got *that* miserable over a woman. Just then he saw Cam walk through the door. Looking at the huge grin and spring in his friend's step, it was hard to reconcile him with the same lovesick fool he'd been just two weeks ago before the wedding.

Robert returned his smile and they met in a hard hug. "You looking good my man! Sit down, I got you a drink already."

Cam sat, still grinning his mega-millions winner smile, "Thanks. I'm feeling good."

When the waitress came they both placed their order quickly, including a couple of shots, which came almost immediately. The two friends raised them up as Robert gave a toast.

"To the newly married Cam!" They both downed the liquor. "So tell me, how's married life?"

"So far so good! You'd be hard pressed to find an unhappy guy after his honeymoon. I think we got that part of marriage figured out at least."

Robert listened as Cam gave him the cliff notes of his trip, glad that everything had worked out for his friend in the end. "That's cool. I think your wedding will go down as one for the books. I had no clue I was coming to Vegas for that."

"Yeah, it was dope. We had a good time partying afterwards too."

"I'm surprised you remember, we were all tossing drinks back like water," Robert reminded him.

"True. I think the adrenaline of the whole thing kept my mind pretty sharp. Plus we left early to uh...work off some of the alcohol."

"Yeah *I* know." And just like that Robert's mind was brought back to him using sex to clear his alcohol muddled brain as well. By the time he and Mika had gone a couple of vigorous, sweaty rounds before passing out on the twisted sheets, he had probably been sober. The two had stayed another hour in the club after Cam left. Downing a few more shots while dancing with each other and strangers. Robert had only suggested they call it a night due to a guy getting extremely handsy with Mika, both on and off the dance floor.

Cam interrupted his thoughts by saying, "We're both glad you and Mika were able to be there. Honestly, it meant a lot to us."

"Anytime my brother, you know I got your back."

"I'm assuming you had no problems checking out, or with your flight home?" Cam asked.

"None at all." If he didn't count waking up naked with an angry woman ordering him from the room. Especially when just hours before she'd been using that mouth to give him different orders, which he'd been *happy* to comply with. "We both got on the plane. That Mika is a trip though."

"Yeah she is, but you got to admit she's fun as hell. Andrea was excited to get back and talk to her. I had to take Andrea's phone while we were gone, so she wouldn't be tempted to reply to some of the crazy texts Mika sent."

Cam left out that once he'd taken the phone and told Mika to stop texting, he'd actually initiated some of the sexcapades she'd been sending. He really needed to make good on his promise to buy her a really nice gift.

Robert let an ironic smile slip on his face before he thought better of it. He was not surprised she'd had the audacity to bother a couple who were honeymooning. He also figured the two women had probably talked in the last week. He waited to see if Cam would mention him and Mika sleeping together. He figured his friend wouldn't miss a chance to call him on it. That's *if* she'd told Andrea. When Cam just continued to eat, he threw out a line.

"Mika didn't mention anything to Andrea about Vegas?"

Cam looked up from his steak confused. "Not really. She told Andrea she had a great time with the celebration and all. You know the usual. Why? Was there something else?"

"Naw, guess not. She was cozying up with someone at the club after you guys left. I just wondered if she'd taken her celebration any further..." He let his question trail off, keeping his voice faintly bored.

Cam chuckled. "Well that doesn't surprise me. She's a natural flirt. Wouldn't shock me either if she took some lucky bastard back to her room."

"Lucky?"

"Yeah. What man wouldn't be lucky to have a hot, willing woman pick him up while in Vegas? Come on man! I know she rubs you the wrong way but even *you* can't deny she's a sexy woman. A little wild around the edges and likely the same in bed."

Cam's assumption would be right. "I suppose she's hot...just not really my type."

Cam narrowed his eyes at his longtime friend. "So you've said before."

Robert didn't like the introspective way Cam was looking at him, so he deflected. "What would your wife say if she heard you describing her best friend like this?"

Cam laughed outright, shaking his head. "That I have a damn good memory, as those were the words she used to describe her once. Andrea and Mika are like sisters, scratch that they *are* sisters. Which means she's my sister now. That's how I think of her. The mischievous, trouble making little sister I never had."

8

Robert let the subject drop and turned the conversation towards other things. One of his skills was redirecting and shaping the narrative with people. It was a needed skill in his line of business. He let Cam ramble on about the many changes that needed to take place for him and Andrea to combine their households. Not needing to do much to uphold his end of the conversation, he let his mind wonder.

Was it slight annoyance he felt at Mika not mentioning their tryst to her best friend? Was he being ridiculous? They *were* adults, so he really didn't expect her to go around sharing all her sexual exploits. Then again, if what Cam said was accurate, they were closer than friends. Would someone texting a person on their honeymoon, hesitate to mention hooking up with a guy at the wedding celebration? Probably not, *if* she thought it was important. The fact that she hadn't thought it worth mentioning grated on his nerves for some reason.

All this made him scrap his original plan to ask Cam for her number. That he'd even thought about reaching out had truly surprised him. He honestly didn't like the woman. She was highly self-assured, pushy and opinionated in the extreme. To say she was a natural flirt was an understatement. She was a woman well aware of her looks and body, and what both did to the opposite sex. He'd watched her use those charms shamelessly throughout the night as they'd hit up three different clubs. Even getting a taxi driver to wave his fare. True, it had been a short ride as the guys hailed the car only to spare the ladies another walk. Still who ever heard of a cabbie turning down money? And in Vegas no less!

Mika was trouble just waiting to happen. He definitely didn't need a headache like that, not even to keep his sheets warm for a month or two. And that's all it would be. A short interlude, until they both tired of the other. Plus Cam had just reiterated how important this woman was to his

9

wife and thus him. Getting between her thick thighs again wasn't worth potentially causing a rift between Andrea and by default Cam.

Cam would and *should* put his wife first in all things. That change in their relationship was a reality now. Which meant he was playing with fire in more ways than one. It was a good bet it wouldn't end well if he and Mika got together, their personalities being what they were. And no matter what most women said, they wanted a long-term relationship, or at least more than the occasional hook-up. He was *not* the long-term type. If his status ever changed he couldn't see it being with Mika Harrison. So that settled it. He'd follow the golden rule of "what happens in Vegas stays in Vegas."

Chapter Two

Mika let out a grunt then a sigh, as she shifted the box she'd just finished taping to the side. It was late September, and Michigan weather had graced them with an Indian Summer. Thank god for air conditioning as they were packing the second floor of Andrea's house. Swiping an errant curl off her forehead, along with a little sweat Mika asked, "So have you decided to sell or what?"

Andrea plopped down on the bed exhausted. She and Cam had come by Friday night to pack, and here she was again with Mika the next day. Since the movers were coming on Monday it was a sure bet she'd be here tomorrow as well.

"Andrea?"

"Sorry. Between the heat, packing and planning for the move I'm a scatterbrain. Thanks again for finding time to help."

"You're welcome, and you owe me some pizza and wine to replace all the calories I'm burning. I forgot how hard packing and moving could be. I haven't done any of this since college."

"Done! You're cheap labor. We've decided to keep the place and rent it out. I'm thinking a short rental. If we don't get enough traffic that way we can do Airbnb. Particularly since it's close to the airport. Extra income to invest."

"That sounds like a great plan. You've always been money savvy."

"Yeah, but Cam and Robert take it to another level."

Mika's head snapped around, but luckily Andrea had her eyes closed. "What does Robert have to do with it?"

"Well you know he's a financial investor. He's handled Cam's investments since they met years ago."

"Ahh, I get it. He's responsible for Cam being able to buy all your wonderful jewelry."

"Yep, a big part actually. Cam's convinced me to take the extra from the rental and let Robert handle it." Andrea got up, stretched and went back to removing items from the closet. How did one person accumulate all this crap? "You should let him invest for you as well."

"Who Cam?"

"No, Robert. Now who's slow? You should talk to him about setting up an account, get a better return on your money."

"I *do* invest you know," Mika told her.

"Barely. With as much as you make, you could be investing a lot more and getting better returns if you let a professional do it."

"Ugh, he's the last person I'd ask for help," Mika mumbled.

"What? Why not?"

Mika turned to see Andrea looking at her with genuine curiosity. Shit, what should she say now? She hadn't told her bestie that she and the best man had done the old tango in the sheets routine. Or that she had a keen dislike for the man.

"Am I missing something?" Andrea asked when Mika didn't answer.

"No...I just don't know him like that to trust him with my money."

"I get it. But he's solid. You should really think about it," Andrea said, turning back around.

"Yeah okay. I will. But I have plenty of money."

"I know...and you'll go see Robert if you want to *keep* it," Andrea scolded.

Two hours later found both women downstairs devouring the delivered pizza and drinking.

"Thanks again girl. I'll have to take you to dinner as a real payment. I hate it's only our second time catching up since the wedding, and I have you doing manual labor."

Mika waved the comment away as she chewed a string of cheese. "Honestly, its fine. I'm not married like you. Not like anyone is waiting for me at home. I had nothing else to do."

Andrea furrowed her brow at the hint of wistfulness in her friend's tone. "Well then, we need to get you hitched."

"No thanks. Don't be that happily married friend who tries to fix everyone else up."

"I wouldn't do that!"

Mika gave her a side eye. "Mmm-hmm. I know you can be a schemer when you want to be."

"This is true," Andrea said grinning. "Tell you what, we'll work with your current roster before I go sticking my nose in."

"My current roster is empty."

"Come on...I know you usually keep a few on the bench. You telling me there isn't *anyone* you'd like to revisit?"

Mika actually thought about that question between a few sips of wine. As the silence grew, she frowned. "No. Nobody comes to mind actually. Which is fine by me. I'm not ready to take the plunge yet. I *would* like my dating life to ramp back up though. I think I'm getting bored."

Andrea didn't say anything for a moment, just studied her bestie. Mika was fiddling with her earrings while stuffing her face with food. "Ahh, I get it you do seem to have a lot of pent up energy. But be serious, you can have sex whenever. What are you looking for in a guy for a long-term relationship?"

"That's the point. I'm *not* looking...well not really." And Mika wasn't. Long-term relationships seemed like a lot of work.

"Whatever, neither was I. I know you eventually want to get married and for that to happen you need to start with a *real relationship*. Quick give me five things you want in your Mr. Right!"

"Okay, he needs to be...umm adventurous, outgoing, fun, manly and at least 6'2."

"Three of those things mean basically the same thing. Think deeper than that. Does he need to be well off?" Andrea asked knowing Mika's background.

Mika twisted her mouth and shook her head. "Not really. I mean he needs to be taking care of himself, but I don't want a career obsessed man. Nor do I *need* one. I have money and money isn't everything."

"Well what do you want *besides* fun in a mate?"

"Look Andrea, I don't know. Not everyone can nab a good looking, funny, caring and successful guy like you did," Mika said standing up and brushing pizza crumbs off her jeans, before grabbing her purse. "Maybe in five to ten years I'll run into my own unicorn. Thanks for the pizza, but it's late and I'm beat. I'll talk to you later!"

Mika yelled the last as she was walking out the door, Andrea's mouth still hanging open from her outburst. Reaching the car, she blew out the breath she was holding and let her head fall onto the steering wheel. She had no clue why she'd just blown up at Andrea. She couldn't be happier that her friend *had* in fact found a black unicorn, she deserved it. Yet here she was, lashing out like a bitter shrew. When her phone buzzed, she pulled it out to read the text.

Andrea: Not sure what happened. Sorry I upset you
Andrea: Still, let me know you get home safely

Great. That made her feel like even more of an ass. Why did she have a friend who took the high road more often than not? She could have at least called me a bad name or two.

Mika: I will
Mika: I'm sorry too. Wasn't you, was me :(

Putting on her seatbelt she pulled out the driveway and started for home, deep in thought. Could she be jealous of her friend? Maybe. After all who wouldn't be a tad bit? Andrea had gotten that random meeting that turned into a whirlwind romance. The shit that people wrote books and poems about. At the same time Mika wasn't sure she was ready for a heavy relationship. The thought of having to put someone else first made her cringe. All for a fifty/fifty chance they wouldn't cheat on you, be secretly gay, or heaven forbid both.

Maybe it had been Andrea's implication that my relationships weren't "real". Did she have a point? While Andrea had rarely dated when she did, it often morphed into a longer arrangement. While she on the other hand dated often and the potential mates morphed into thin air. The longest relationship she'd ever had was eight months long. Was that right? While sitting at a light she mentally went back to college and worked her way up. She didn't like the answer she came up with. She'd only had about three relationships to reach six months. Not realizing it since she usually moved on to the next fairly quickly. Casual dating taking the place of forming lasting relationships.

"Well, damn..."

What kind of guy could make her want to settle down? She wasn't sure, as she honestly didn't spend much time thinking about it. What she wanted was someone she was passionate about, and who felt the same about her. Someone who liked her for all her quirky habits and wouldn't try to change her into a Stepford wife. All the successful black men seemed to be stiff and dull. As if they didn't know how to relax outside the office. She wanted the perfect man for *her*. While she might be sketchy on exactly what that looked like, she felt certain she hadn't met him yet.

Chapter Three

"Explain to me again why you waited so late to ask her?" Cam asked as he walked past, pulling on his shirt.

Andrea gave his disappearing skin an appreciative look before shaking her head. "Well I probably would have thirty minutes ago, if *someone* hadn't ambushed my shower. I told you this way she has less time to think about it."

"What if she has plans?"

"She doesn't. Unless she added some since yesterday...which is possible. About to call and find out now."

Mika sat at home in her favorite chair almost finished painting her nails hunter green, while watching "Wifey Club of Charlotte". Why she watched this trashy show she didn't know. It reminded her of her cousins, which wasn't a good thing. She figured she could get another episode in before the game came on. She loved mid-October as she knew the rivalry of Michigan vs. State would be an entertaining game. Most years she went to a viewing party given by friends or colleagues. She'd even randomly picked a sports bar a few times and joined the animated crowds.

Occasionally, she had dragged Andrea to a few events over the years. Her friend didn't mind sports now and then, but said the craziness of this particular game annoyed her. Mika agreed it could get wild, which was why she would be screaming out her lungs in the privacy of her own home this year. Her phone rang just as a lady on "WCOC" was getting overpriced champagne thrown in her face.

"Hello." She hadn't even looked at the caller ID. Her eyes still glued to the screen as a table was flipped. Seriously, why were these people not banned from all nice places by now?

"Hey! What you doing?"

"Watching these fancy waiters trying to break up a fight. Girl they don't get paid to do all that! I'd quit."

"Don't tell me you're watching that crap again."

"Yeah. Figured I'd catch up on my DVR before the game came on. What's up?"

"You want to go to a watch party with us? A friend of Cam's is hosting."

Mika gave Andrea her full attention now that a commercial was on. "Huh? I thought you hated this game."

"True, but I figured since Cam wanted to go..."

"Ha, part of your marriage duties! I'm becoming old like you, I honestly didn't want all the drama this year. I told you that's why I'm watching solo."

"I know, I know. But this is a small gathering maybe twenty people. Right Camden?"

Mika heard him agree in the background before she spoke up again. "Yeah, but..."

"Come on, no buts. We can hang out and you can wile out for your team at the same time. We'll even pick you up, so you can drink as much as you want." When Mika still hemmed and hawed Andrea quickly added in a whisper, "Please go! That way I'll know at least one other female there. Hell, I don't even know if there'll *be* other women."

"I really doubt Cam would take you to an all male party," Mika said dryly. "Fine. I'll go."

"Yay, you're the best! We're on our way. Give us about thirty-five minutes."

"That's fine, you know I'm already dressed."

"I know it! You'll have fun in a smaller setting."

'Yeah, yeah hurry up, the game starts in about an hour."

In the time it took them to get to her house she freshened up, then hunted up a couple of extra props. Grabbing a jacket and a bottle of wine as a gift to the host, she was ready and waiting when Andrea texted they were outside. Locking up, she jogged her way out to the car and got in the back.

"What's up people! Thanks sexy Cam for driving!"

"Not a problem Ms. Trouble."

Conversation flowed easily between the three as it always did, making Mika glad she'd come out. She'd gotten used to being the third wheel while the two had dated. Overall it didn't bother her because she liked Cam so much. He was like the indulgent older brother she'd never had. Easy to talk to, quick to laugh and 250% in love with her friend.

Funny how time seemed to go more quickly when someone else drove. In no time they were pulling into a curved driveway. They stood outside the home's door still chatting, as they waited for it to be answered. She finally noticed neither had on anything that represented a team. "Cam you went neutral too? I'm disappointed in you. Pick a side!"

"Nope, I have no skin in this fight. I'll leave all that craziness up to you and Robert. Though I *do* put a small bet randomly on a team each year, just for the hell of it."

Mika face twisted hearing *that* name. It had taken her almost a full month to stop having random flashbacks of that man. So imagine her dismay as the door opened and there he stood.

* * *

Mika saw the surprise in Robert's eyes as well. As he and Cam greeted each other she whispered to Andrea, "You didn't tell me he would be here."

"Well it's his house party." Looking confused Andrea asked, "Does it matter?"

Pressing her lips together Mika turned around and entered the house at Cam's urging. Once they were all inside she tried to get her bearings, as Robert greeted and hugged Andrea. Okay, this wasn't the end of the world. It was probably a given she would run into him from time to time. Though what were the odds, since she'd gone a whole year never meeting him before the wedding? However a married couple *truly* combined their lives, and that meant their friends too. Shit.

Robert stepped up to Mika as their friends took off their coats. He was completely surprised to see her standing in his house, and right now he couldn't decide if he was annoyed or not. "Didn't expect to see you."

"Same here. Andrea didn't say Cam's friend was *you*. I would have stayed home."

"You sure should have, coming in my house wearing all that hideous green."

She snorted looking him up and down. He had on a maize and blue sweatshirt along with a watch with the school's logo. "Whatever. *You* would be backing a losing team like the University of Michigan."

"It's 'Hail to the Victors', all day long baby in this household. I'm a proud alumni."

"Why does that not surprise me. They usually produce boring, fake know-it-alls. *I'm* a legacy of the best, Green and White is the only way to go."

"Both of you give it a rest," Andrea said walking back to them. "Camden why didn't you tell me Robert was a Michigan fanatic?"

"I told you he was a huge sports fan." Cam wasn't bothered by the other pair's banter. That's what these parties were for. So opposing teams could trash talk at each other the whole night.

Andrea took the wine out of Mika's hand and shoved it into Robert's. "Here, she brought a peace offering."

"Nope for him it's going to be a consolation prize," Mika taunted, walking past Robert to join the rest of the gathering.

Returning from putting away the wine and his new guests' coats, Robert found Mika sitting between his two younger cousins, both idiots already grinning. He took a seat off to the side so he could watch TV and keep an eye on the minx that was currently touching Devon's knee. She seemed to have no problem relaxing with other men just not him. She probably wasn't used to a guy not falling all over themselves for her. Like Darrell was doing now by jumping up to go get her something to drink from the kitchen. He also noticed a few of the other men giving her more than a casual look. More power to them. It was clear *their* mutual dislike of each other mirrored this game's rivalry...instant and strong.

Mika found herself having a good time despite the fact she was in *his* house. Everyone was lively, friendly and into the game. Well mostly. Out of the twenty-two people that sat or chatted around Robert's generous living room, there were about seven other women besides her and Andrea. It was obvious three were with boyfriends or husbands, and Mika couldn't tell about the other four. They all seemed to be well known and from pieces of conversation she caught this wasn't the first year they'd watched the game here. From the side-eye looks a few were giving her she figured they were "friends" of the host.

She found it interesting that he remained friendly with *any* of his past lovers. He hadn't seemed the type. He struck her as overall rigid, like the type when a relationship was over, it was *completely* over. For her part she paid the women no mind, as they were civil enough. To her it was clear the women had come to get his attention, *not* to watch the game. However not her monkey, not her problem.

Chapter Four

Mika would give him this, he threw a great party with excellent food and plenty of drinks. She was enjoying clowning with his guests. There was another State alumni and a few State fans in the house. She was surprised at how much she liked his cousins. They were nowhere near as stuffy as he was, and they were almost as fine too. A much better combination she thought, having fun flirting with the two. So much fun it seemed like she blinked and they were in the fourth quarter. The game was looking like it would be close.

Robert was mildly pissed. His team was close but not winning, and he was tired of watching Mika flirt with his cousins and charm the rest of the people in the room. She'd quickly become the center of attention. Between her enthusiasm for the game and what she had on, he wasn't surprised. She sported a white long-sleeved shirt, covered by a green and white State jersey that clung to her ample chest and curvy hips like a mini-dress, stopping right below her ass. Skin-tight white leggings traced her long legs, ending in stiletto boots with the Michigan State logo on them. Where in the hell had she found those?

Trying not to grind his teeth and mess up the great smile his mother had paid for with expensive braces, he noticed Darrell head out the room. Robert got up and took the spot vacated seat. He noticed she tensed up as he sat down, taking some small satisfaction in her unease since her presence had done the same to him all night.

She ignored him for almost ten seconds before turning and putting her finger in his face. "Your team sucks."

Robert swiped the large green foam #1 away. "Really? All we need to do is keep them from advancing to the next down. Then it's about one minute left, and we only need a field goal to win."

"That's a lot *y'all* need to do against a team already kicking your butt." Mika watched as Darrell came back, throwing his hands up at Robert taking his seat. The man in question just looked at him and nodded his head to the left, as if telling him to take a hike. Robert definitely made no move to get up. Darrell grumbled but moved on. "That was rude."

"It's my house, I sit where I want."

"You're supposed to be nice and defer to your guests...just in case no one ever told you that." They both heard Devon on her other side snicker.

"Does my conduct not suit Miss Manners? Besides, he's no guest just family. The *deference* he gets is eating my food and drinking my liquor."

She whipped her head around and narrowed her eyes at him. "Whatever. Just because your team is about to lose doesn't mean you need to take your aggression out on folks." As he watched the green pom-pom antennas swaying on top of her head, he wondered how he could find himself wanting to shake her and kiss her at the same time. Between the headpiece and the foam finger she should have looked goofy or flat-out stupid. Instead the headgear on top of her wild curly hair looked adorable, while the rest of her just looked outright sexy. Cheers in the room brought his focus back to the game. He was the only fool not watching the screen to see that U of M defense had done its job, and the ball was turned over with fifty seconds left. He turned back to his adversary once the broadcast cut to commercial.

"You want to make a wager on the game?" He saw her eyes light up with interest at the question.

"Hmm, depends on what we betting. On the unrealistic chance that State loses, what do you want?"

He aimed a smile her way for the first time that evening. "A case of Auchentoshan American Oak Scotch Whisky. It's about $40 a bottle."

Mika just lifted a brow. "What are you an alcoholic?"

"I'll use it for my next party. Maybe next year when Michigan will be beating your team *again*."

"Okay...whatever. And when *I* win you can have a case of Diva Sangiovese by Naked Winery delivered to me."

He snorted at the name of wine, though it fit her to a tee. "Bet." They shook on it and he tried to ignore the shock of electricity that seemed to go straight to his balls. He saw her eyes widen before she jerked her hand away and faced the TV. Good to see he wasn't the only one feeling the attraction.

The whole house focused on the remaining seconds of the game. Yells ensued! While threats to the coach, players and their family members were screamed at the TV from both sides. As U of M struggled to get the ball down the field. Then just like that it was over. The field goal kick was blocked. State had won.

Robert watched as Mika celebrated the win, jumping around like a little kid, before running to embrace the other State fans. Robert shook his head at her *and* the lost game, standing up to take the jokes that he knew were coming. He took it more gracefully than normal, mostly because he was only half-listening. His eyes busy tracking Mika around the room. He eventually saw her talking to Cam and Andrea, who had their coats in their hands. He frowned as he saw them pointing Mika down the hall. Probably directing her to where she could find her coat. Making a split-second decision, he picked up the phone she'd left on the living room table and followed her.

Mika danced down the hall following Cam's directions. She walked into what seemed to be a den/library combination and sure enough saw several jackets and fall coats tossed over a loveseat. Picking up her State jacket, she slipped it on before taking in the room. Like the rest of the house it was tastefully done. Not fussy, but stylish with a contemporary feel to it. She was actually surprised considering whose house it was. Mika had expected over the top pretentiousness, something to let everyone know he was "high-level".

As much as she had enjoyed the game and the company, she was ready to leave. The undercurrent of tension between her and Robert the whole night was nothing compared to that jolt of sexual recognition that had zinged through her palm *and* body when they'd sealed the bet. In her brain there was a neon sign clearly yelling, "Danger, Mika Harrison!" Whatever else she might be she wasn't a complete idiot. It was time to go! Still she made her way to his bookshelves, taking a quick peek at what he read.

Robert entered the room to see her lightly running a finger along book spines. He stepped inside, closing the door behind him. When she turned around at the soft click, the smile on her face faded.

"Are you being nosy?" He asked.

"Just getting my coat and looking around. What are *you* doing?" Her eyes flickered to the door he'd purposely closed.

"Bringing you your phone. The one you carelessly left on the table." He held it out and watched her shoulders relax as she walked over to him.

"Thanks actually. I'm horrible about keeping up with my phone sometimes."

She went to take it from him which he allowed, before wrapping his big hand around hers. Her eyes snapped to his face before he stepped in, closing the distance between them.

"You're welcome." After a beat of silence he continued. "What are we going to do about this Mika?"

"This *what?* You can start by releasing my phone and getting out of my space...*Robert.*" She tried tugging free.

"You know what I'm talking about." He proved his point by stroking her hand with his thumb, watching her lips part before they tightened. "This sexual attraction. Neither of us can blame it on alcohol this time."

"First, I *still* don't know what you're talking about. Two, speak for yourself. I indulged in plenty of your fine alcoholic beverages, and if you—"

He had enough of watching her lips deny the situation. Swooping in for a kiss that would not only quiet her, but would prove his point. He instantly felt her yield against him as he tilted her head up, tangling his hand in the mass of hair he'd admired earlier. He let go of the phone pulling her waist against his body. Sure she would feel the *proof* of his attraction.

Mika forgot what they'd been debating the moment his full firm lips brushed hers. She wasn't thinking. She *was* feeling his hardness against her stomach, the firm muscles on his back as she circled her arms around him. And damn him but she felt the masterful way he used his hand in her hair to deepen the kiss.

His tongue seemingly sweeping every inch of her mouth. He took her breath away, and she was starting to think maybe breathing was overrated? Everything was on automatic, and thank God for that as some part of her brain heard Andrea's voice in the hall. She jerked back before pushing past him, so she was closest to the door when it opened.

"There you are, I thought you might have gotten lost..." Andrea trailed off as she took in the pair. "Oh, was Robert helping you?"

"Nope." Robert turned to face them. "I was returning her phone. Didn't want her leaving without it."

"Yeah, you know I seem to misplace my phone at least once a week. Anyway I'm ready to head out," Mika corroborated.

"You guys don't have to leave so early. Cam you know the party usually goes for another few hours."

Andrea looked guilty before speaking up. "Sorry. I've reached my limit on football and smack talking for the day."

"The wife is ready to go." Cam still got a kick out of saying the title. "I *did* win a Benjamin on the game from the loss," Cam said grinning.

"Oh you bet against my team? Then it's definitely time for you to exit my house."

As Robert and Cam started bantering back and forth, the group left the room and made their way to the front door. Opening it Mika enjoyed the cool air rushing over her heated skin. She knew it was a mistake looking back around when Robert immediately caught her eye.

"Mika, you never answered my question."

"Sure I did. You can have my wine delivered anytime in the evening or on the weekend."

When he looked like he was about to speak again and damn an audience, she rushed on. "Great party! Andrea and I will be in the car, it's chilly." She dragged Andrea forward before Robert could say anything else. Cam following a few minutes later. As they drove to drop her off her mind went where it shouldn't. Back to that room, wrapped in the arms of a man who stepped on *every* nerve she had. Which equaled a BI. In this case a *very* **B**ad **I**dea for everyone involved.

Chapter Five

The last Friday in October found Mika happy to finally be back home. She'd gone out with a few co-workers for drinks after work, and was just getting in close to eight. She left her heeled boots haphazardly at the door and headed to her bedroom. While they hadn't had an early snow, the weather *had* taken a major dip in temperature. Taking a quick hot shower to warm up before throwing on some pajamas. She settled in for the night and scanned Netflix to see what was on.

Picking a comedy, she stretched out to eat the dessert she'd brought back from the bar. Her sweet tooth was going to kill her one day. Or at least add weight in undesirable places in a few years. Ten minutes into the show her phone pinged. She thought about not even checking it, she was "peopled-out" right about now. Then again checking it didn't mean she had to reply.

She unlocked the phone and blinked a couple of times. Yes she'd had three cocktails, but she'd eaten a full dinner with them. She wasn't drunk *or* delusional last time she checked. Yet the message remained on her screen.

Robert: Call me

What in all the nine levels of hell was this? She'd spent the week since the game ruthlessly shutting down any thoughts of him. Now he was somehow texting her, *and* had the audacity to give her orders. Of course she'd wondered would he try to reach out after that kiss. However she hadn't really expected it, and sure enough nothing had happened until now. She couldn't imagine he thought they were a good idea, any more than she did. Mika doubted he had such a tough time getting laid that he would pursue her when she wasn't interested. Well okay...her *body* was, but her *mind* wanted nothing to do with him.

Mika: No

When no response came she relaxed and ate the last bite on her fork. Two minutes later, her phone rang. She closed her eyes and thought about not answering, but then decided this was stupid, she was tired of running from this man. It wasn't in her nature to do so, particularly where men were concerned. She'd tell him to take a hike, and that would be the end of it.

Mika answered the phone. "Who dis?"

"Stop it. You saw my name on the caller ID."

"What do you want?" She made her voice disinterested.

"We need to talk."

"That's an opinion I don't share," she volleyed back.

"So you don't think we need to address the fact that we slept together in Vegas? Or that we're still strongly attracted to each other now?"

"No to both. Vegas was Vegas...shit happens," she added a hint of steel to her voice. The tone she used at work from time to time, when she had to check a condescending ass-hole. "There is no law that says *you* have to act on the attraction *you* think is present."

"Just me huh?"

"Apparently. I'm good over here." Mika listened to the long pause of silence from the other end. Maybe he would let it go. He was a man, which meant he was prideful. Maybe he wasn't used to being turned down and would want to cut his losses. Instead, she heard a low chuckle over the line that had her holding her breath.

"Okay...I see you want to make this more complicated than it has to be. So be it. We'll talk later."

"There's nothing else to talk abo—" She heard the click of the phone and looked to her screen, incredulous as the "call ended" message flashed. "That man's ego is so damn inflated! It's a wonder he doesn't just float off!"

Tossing the phone on the couch she refused to let him ruin her night. Reaching for her drink she grimaced when her hand came back only holding a water bottle. She was actively trying to cut down on her in-home drinking. She'd prefer to be sipping on something more than H2O right about now. Mika tried to stop the conversation from replaying in her head, but it was near impossible. Almost an hour later and she was still thinking about it.

Just who did he think he was? First trying to order her around, then refusing to take no for an answer. Did he really think he laid pipe *that* good? That one night with him would render a woman incapable of not sleeping with him again? So what if she couldn't keep her eyes off him when they were in the same room? An electric touch and a stupid hot kiss didn't mean she was controlled by her hormones. Already edgy she let out a little groan followed by a small scream of frustration when the doorbell rang.

* * *

Robert admitted hanging up had been petty and done partially out of anger. Turning the light off in the bathroom he grabbed what he needed and left. He couldn't say he was a man with a lot of patience outside of work. Even *at* work he could be a bit of an asshole, as he convinced people to part with their money and entrust it to him. People preferred confidence and competence at the end of the day, when dealing with large sums of money or their life savings. He had a finite amount of real patience, which he saved and used for his close friends and family. As of right now he'd used up all the patience Mika Harrison was going to get.

For sure he'd taken his *shot* a number of times in life and been rejected. That was part of life, hell part of being a man. He took his hits on the chin and kept it moving. But he'd be damned if she would dismiss him over the phone like he wasn't worth at least a conversation. How she could outright deny that there was a spark between them, he'd never know. If they never hooked up again so be it. But they needed to clear the air for any future run-ins they had. Robert didn't believe in letting stuff fester and he wasn't about to start now. Which is how he found himself standing outside her door fifty minutes later. He rang the bell a second time and waited. Finally, he heard some movement behind the door.

"Who is it?"

He was leaning down to the peephole already, but in a dry voice answered, "Open the door. If you leave me standing outside too long you know someone will call the police."

Shit. He had a point. Someone in her nice, pricey Canton suburbs *would* call the police. They would think he was casing the place, no matter how nice his car or clothes might be. She reluctantly opened the door but blocked the entrance.

"Would serve you right if I let them. What do you want?" She looked him over. There he stood, a tall, sexy and aggravated man outside her door. He was dressed in jeans and a nice t-shirt, with an excellent blazer thrown over it all. He shook his head, then slid past her into the house. Closing the door against her better judgement as she was letting the cold air in, she faced him. Crossing her arms under her braless breasts, she saw Robert's eyes track the movement then remain on her chest. Annoyed that her nipples started to harden she spat out.

"Why the hell are you here? At my house, uninvited?"

"You wouldn't talk over the phone. So I decided to come here and see if you can ignore this face-to-face."

"Oh, so *this* is how you react when you don't get your way...noted." Disgusted Mika took a few steps further into the house before thinking better of it. Instead she rounded on him, hands on hips. "Just how the hell did you know where I live in the first place? I doubt Cam or Andrea would have given you my address. At least not without telling me."

"The same way I texted you. I put my name and number in your phone before I gave it back to you. Got the address from looking at your gps app. Phones automatically mark your home address."

"What the fuck, Robert!" She threw her hands up. "Do you stalk much?"

"I wouldn't go that far. I view getting the address as information I needed to send you the wine you won off me."

"And I guess it never occurred for you to *ask*?"

"Quicker to just get it myself. You seem to have a tiresome habit of *not* answering my questions. Besides now maybe you'll think twice before leaving your phone unattended."

Mika forgot about keeping her distance, walking forward to poke her finger into his chest. "Where *is* my wine since we speaking on it? That should have been the *only* reason for you to ever to show up at my door."

"It's on its way, should arrive early next week. But that's not why I'm here and you know it." He grabbed her finger as it went to poke him again.

Mika took a step back and he matched it with one step forward. "Why *exactly* are you here? Besides your perturbing stalking tendencies."

"To finish our conversation."

"*You* hung up in a fit." Why was she allowing him to still hold her finger? Wetting her lips, she saw his eyes jump to them like a magnet. His own lips tightening in response.

She felt the air around them change, and more softly she said, "You didn't come here to talk."

He let her finger drop, reaching up instead to rub his thumb back and forth on her bottom lip. His voice came out low and aroused when he answered. "I did...but I'm thinking we can talk after."

"After...what?" She snuck her tongue out and gave his thumb a quick lick, followed by a teasing nip.

"Shit, after I get inside you again." He lifted her up in his arms eliciting a startled yelp of surprise as she hurried to wrap her arms around his neck. "Tell me which way, before we end up taking care of business on these nice wood floors of yours."

The time to tell him to get the hell out was now. Instead Mika found herself pointing down the hall to her spare bedroom. She didn't think his patience would make it upstairs. Now that it was decided she relaxed against him. Lifting her head slightly to lick and nibble along his neck. She was tired. Tired of fighting the sexual pull to him. Tired of rejecting what they both wanted and denying the male carrying her in his strong arms. Their brief physical touches already had her needy. She wanted to lick more than his thumb and neck before the night was over.

Chapter Six

Robert waited until he entered the bedroom before letting her slide down his body. Once she was on her own two feet, he took her mouth in a maddening kiss full of need. For weeks, no scratch that almost two months he'd wanted to have this woman underneath him again. His hands were actually shaking a bit, as he grabbed her ass and pulled her against his aching penis. This woman defied, frustrated and excited him all at the same time. If he had been thinking right he'd have his ass at home. Instead, all he could think about were her hands impatiently pulling his shirt from his pants.

He released her so he could shrug out of his blazer and toe off his footwear. As soon as he did she was pushing his t-shirt up toward his head. He took over finishing the job, and she wasted no time putting her lips to his skin. Licking and kissing his nipples as her fingernails scraped along his love handles towards his zipper. He shivered at the sensation and dragged her head up for another ravenous kiss. *This* was the woman he remembered from Vegas. Greedy and bold, taking what she wanted *from* him and *for* herself.

He nipped the inside of her bottom lip in retaliation for her nails and felt her smile against his lips. His hands went back to her hips before scowling at the feel of material against his fingers. He wanted skin to skin contact. Putting space between them, he pulled her shirt up and over, covering her breasts with his hands. Robert became instantly harder at the feel of her flesh, so soft yet firm as he shaped and squeezed. He pulled at her nipple, thrilled by the moan she gave him in return. Her breasts were large for her frame, giving her that coke bottle shape when you added in her thick hips and ass. He normally didn't covet more than a handful or so, but looking down at her all he saw was a bountiful meal, and he was a *very* hungry man.

Dipping his head he brought her flesh up to his mouth and latched on, pulling strongly from the start. He felt her knees give out before she anchored herself using his waist. Right before he felt his pants and boxers being pushed down his hips, then to his knees, before her warm hand wrapped tightly around his member. He feasted while she stroked—she stroked while he feasted. When he'd had his fill he begin nipping his way up her chest to her neck. Finally he glided her pants down and once they cleared her butt they slid to the ground, where she kicked them off.

He moved his hand to palm her center. "First no bra, now no panties. Got me thinking maybe you were expecting me," he said cockily.

"Only in your stalker dreams. I'm not sure there's enough space in this room for me, you, and your ego," Mika stated, still stroking his length rubbing his tip with her thumb spreading his pre-cum around.

Robert chuckled and finished pushing his jeans down his legs. He took a few extra seconds to remove two condoms from his back pocket, letting her see them before he tossed them towards the bed. "I have no doubt that what I got, will fit perfectly *in you.*" Saying so he slid two of his long fingers inside her.

Mika's reply to his bold statement was cut off as she felt him inside her. Her head fell back and he sucked hard at the fragile skin near her collarbone, while simultaneously moving in and out of her. Her whole body felt electrified! How could the same person she should have slammed the door on, make her slick and wet in mere minutes?

When he passionately took her mouth again while circling his thumb against her clit, her legs finally buckled as she clenched and came around his fingers. He barely let her come down from the high before he was maneuvering her to the bed. When they fell onto it they instantly devoured each other. Hands, tongues, and fingers roamed everywhere. Teeth nipped, tongues licked, nails grazed and hands gripped...hot eager flesh. All of it was too much, and not enough at the same time.

Apparently he was having the same thoughts, as Mika heard the crackle of a wrapper and opened her eyes to watch him. The man was *fine*. His dark-brown, umber skin rippled as his muscles moved. His stomach was flat and firm, the definition of abs etched across it. His shoulders smooth and wide hunched over as he focused on protecting them. He was so delicious and sexy that just looking at him handle himself made her throat go dry, and her inner walls flex in anticipation.

Finally he was sheathed and raised his eyes to hers. She crooked her finger toward him opening her legs in invitation, and Robert wasted no time accepting. Fitting his hips high between her thighs, entering her slowly as he went. Her lashes fluttered but they never lost eye contact. She loved the feel of him—thick, long, and hard—as he inched his way inside. Her breath hitching as he kept going until every inch filled her. Only then did he close his eyes as an involuntary shiver ran through his whole body.

It was one, two, three beats before his eyes opened, staring at her with an intense focus and desire so blazing that her skin flushed with color. Robert begin to move, sure and powerful. He felt so *good*! Soon he was lifting her knees, dragging her even closer to his pumping hips. He went in deep and paused, lifting her left leg almost straight until it rested along his chest and shoulder. When he leaned forward at the new angle she moaned. When he started moving she didn't know *what* sounds were coming out of her mouth. They were both breathing hard, each straining against the other, reaching for that feeling of completion.

After a few minutes Mika lowered a hand to his hip and pushed, she wanted more than this position could give her. He relented, dropping her leg and leaning in for a kiss before he rolled them over while still connected. Mika took the time to kiss and lick his nipples before she sat up seating herself fully on him. The action made him groan but not as much as when she begin to move her hips, doing a slow grind, working him like a joystick that just happened to be deep inside her. She saw him gritting his teeth right before he threw his head back in pleasure.

She couldn't help the small smile that flitted across her face before she finally started to lift and lower herself on his cock. His head snapped forward so his eyes could watch where their bodies met, as he disappeared inside her body over and over again. She found and took her own pleasure in riding him, controlling the speed and intensity of her thrusts. Her own hands shaping and squeezing her breasts adding to the ecstasy assaulting her body.

When she started speeding up and became wilder, he interceded. First massaging her ass before moving his large hands to cover her breasts. Mika leaned forward hands on his chest while he played with her nipples. Eventually he started to raise his hips to meet her, moving his hands to hold her waist tightly. So tightly she'd have marks on her skin tomorrow. Right now she only cared about the exhilaration she felt.

The sounds of their bodies slapping, moans, groans, and mutterings of their passion were like a symphony to her ears. She started to keen incomprehensible sounds her breathing *and* body shaking. He pulled her down lower, until her breasts dangled over his face. When his lips clamped around a nipple and pulled hard she went over, crying out his name and convulsing all around him.

Her body was *still* having mini-explosions when he kissed away what little breath she had, before reversing their positions. Mouths still fused, he slammed into her several times before he found his own release, shouting as his back arched. She soothed a hand along his sweat-slicked back down to his buttocks, their lust fully and completely spent.

Mika slowly opened her eyes, and looked at the ocean blue walls of her guest bedroom. Rolling to her back and stretching brought her mind into sharper focus, as her body reminded her she'd had energetic sex with Robert Lorde. They'd fallen asleep only for him to wake her around two a.m., with his mouth suckling her breast and his hand delving between her legs. They'd gone another heated round before falling back to sleep exhausted.

Now her enthusiastic partner was nowhere to be seen. Climbing out of bed she didn't see his clothes anywhere either. Blowing out a breath she couldn't say she was surprised. He'd come—pun intended—and gotten what he wanted. If she was being honest what they *both* wanted. Maybe now they'd gotten each other out of their systems so to speak.

Her pj's were scattered about, but she ignored them and left the room. Right now she needed a shower and coffee, and wasn't sure which would be first. Noise in the hall drew her back towards the living room. It was probably just the TV. As she got closer she realized it was coming from the kitchen. Heading to investigate, she stopped in the entryway and saw Robert.

Literally the last thing she ever expected to see in her kitchen. At the moment he stood with his back to her, lining up ingredients on the counter. He had on his jeans, though they sagged *just a bit* as his belt wasn't quite buckled. For some reason he hadn't put his shirt or blazer back on yet. Which left that wonderful skin of his visible. Even from back here, she could see the scratches she'd left on his back. Who was this virtual stranger in her kitchen, she knew very little about him. Except that he was currently successful, Cam's best friend, and an unfortunate alumni of U of M. Oh wait, he was also arrogant beyond belief. She must have made some noise because he turned to look in her direction.

He raised an eyebrow at her presence, and she returned the favor.

"What's all this?" She asked.

"It *will* be breakfast as soon as I cook it. I'm starving. You do know you don't have any real food here?"

"I don't really cook. I get a lot of takeout." He just continued to stare, saying nothing. "What? No crack about me not being able to cook?"

"No. It never occurred to me you could," Robert said easily.

"I feel like I should be offended by that, but I'm not. Why don't you stop staring at me and finish cooking, since you invited yourself to do so."

"Sue the hell out of me if I find it difficult not to stare. You're standing there naked."

Mika closed her eyes and suppressed a groan. She'd forgotten she didn't have a stitch on. Refusing to give him the satisfaction of embarrassing her, she didn't move from her current stance. "Well I live alone, I'm used to walking around in the nude. Besides, I thought you were gone. I didn't expect to find you lurking in my kitchen."

"I was hungry."

"So you said." They both paused. She tried to ignore that he was running his eyes slowly along her body. "Well get to cooking."

40

"I will, if you go put some clothes on. Or did you have something else in mind for breakfast?"

"Nope, sure didn't." She started backing away. "I'll...umm, be back down in a bit. Try not to make a mess."

"Food will be done in about ten. If it's cold then that's on you."

"Fine, whatever...make some coffee while you're at it. I'm dying for a cup."

Robert didn't answer, just shook his head before turning around.

Robert soon heard the faint sounds of feet running up the stairs and let himself relax. He picked up his t-shirt from a kitchen stool and put it on. The more clothes they both had on the better. Maybe he *had* come here last night with the goal of ending up in her bed. And *maybe* he'd done it in the hopes of getting rid of the lust he felt for her. Clearly, that hadn't happened as he found himself still here. Cooking of all things and *still* wanting her badly!

"What the fuck am I doing?" He said out loud and started cracking eggs. In a regular situation he would be gone by now, but they did in fact still need to talk. Now that he'd gotten her to admit their physical attraction was off the charts, they could decide how to handle it.

When he'd woken up he'd intended to suggest they engage in a no strings hook-up for a few months. But seeing her naked as the day she was born and probably just as unconcerned, made him think their better option was to ignore each other whenever possible. That thought was reinforced as she'd stood there confident, with bed-head curls and his fingerprints still showing on her skin. Looking like a sexy woodland nymph, whatever the hell that was. All he knew was that it made him want to test the counter for durability.

Mika did her business then took a quick shower, before throwing on some lounging pants and a light-weight sweater. She considered wearing something with State on it just to irritate him, but thought better of it. For now they were behaving in a fairly civilized manner. As her hair was hopelessly tangled, she'd tossed it in a messy top bun and called it a day. Fifteen minutes later she came down to the smell of coffee and forgot everything else except getting a cup.

Robert sat eating already, her plate and a steaming cup of coffee on the other side of him. She took that first wonderful sip before sitting down and speaking, "Thank you. I only drink coffee in the mornings but it's a must have for me to function. I hate mornings."

"Trust me, I remember."

She dug into the veggie omelet and hash browns he'd prepared. Apparently she'd had some deep in her freezer, huh who knew.

Robert let her eat for a full five minutes before he broke the silence. "So how do you want to handle this?"

"What options are on the table?"

She surprised him by finally talking about this head-on, so he took a moment before he answered. "I see two options. The first is we make last night the very last time we have sex. And try to stay out of each other's way as much as possible."

Looking at him over her coffee mug she remained silent, but flashed two fingers at him.

"Two...we can casually hook-up for the next couple of months until we exhaust this sexual attraction between us."

"How would that work exactly in your mind?" Mika asked, setting her cup down and leaning forward.

"The normal way. Either of us calls the other when we have an itch. If the other person is free and interested we scratch that itch. No obligations, free to see and do whatever you want with others."

"Okay, I'm in." She gave him a quick smile and went back to eating.

He dropped his fork. "Let me get this straight. You have no problem with us having a casual here and there sexual relationship."

"Yes, we might as well." Mika shrugged. "You were right, no use in pretending we're not attracted to each other."

"So, what was all the attitude in Vegas?"

"*That* was me waking up with a virtual stranger in my bed, along with a foggy memory. Right now I would have preferred option one, considering the Andrea and Cam connection. Unfortunately I don't see that working, and I find you satisfactory in bed—"

"Just satisfactory?" Robert interrupted with a grin.

"I see no reason we can't occasionally have sex and go about our business. Until the need dies off, like you said," she went on, as if he hadn't spoken. "I was also freaked out in Vegas because I couldn't remember if we'd used a condom."

He became serious. "We did, both times. You were packing, had a couple at the ready in your purse. I'm clean by the way. I get tested every six months, and I *always* wrap it up."

"That's good to know about the testing. I did remember *everything* by the time I got to the airport. But just so we're super clear, you need to always use a condom with me. I'm one of the rare people who have serious side effects from birth control so I can't take it."

"Noted. Trust, I don't want kids. Hell, if the male contraceptive pill was more tested I would pop them like candy."

His comment surprised a genuine, full belly laugh out of her. He grinned back as they shared their first personal joke.

Chapter Seven

Around two Mika walked past her co-worker Sheila, letting her know she was running an errand and would be back in an hour or so. The beginning of November had seen the weather go from chilly to outright cold. She was bundled up in a coat, gloves and a fashionable scarf, which should be enough to navigate the two or so blocks she was walking. To distract herself from the wind and cold, she thought back on the last two weeks. She had been caught by surprise when Robert called her the Monday after their hook-up. She still wasn't sure *why* he'd called now that she thought about it.

Her cell had rang minutes after she got off a conference call. When she saw it was Robert she did a double take but answered. Curious to see what he wanted.

"Robert...what can I do for you."

"That's a loaded question to ask any man."

"Is it really? But for real though, what's up?"

"Nothing, I thought I'd see how your Monday was going."

Mika didn't really know how to take that, so said the first thing that came to her. "It's a pretty standard Monday, as Monday's go. What about you?"

"The same. If by a standard Monday you mean really busy and hectic."

"If you're so busy why are you calling me?" When silence met her statement she smiled. Got him! Luckily all the good sex he'd gave her, had her in an excellent mood. So

45

she took pity on him and changed the subject. "So...where are my flowers?"

"What?"

Poor thing he actually sounded flabbergasted. "My flowers. Cam sent Andrea flowers after their first night together."

"I would think you'd know my name wasn't Cam after last Saturday," he said dismissively, sounding more like himself.

"I'm very aware of that. Hence, why I have no flowers on my desk."

For a few seconds she heard nothing. Then she heard his amused chuckle come across the line. "I can see you're back to your regular program of being a diva of the first order. I'll talk to you later."

He'd hung up and she'd gone back to work, satisfied she had bested him in their latest verbal joust. Two hours later Sheila guided a delivery man to her door. She signed for the flowers and since Sheila's nosy ass was still standing in her office, opened the wrapping. Revealing a lovely small and simple white vase, with four roses. Two red, one white and one orange.

"Read the card!" Sheila demanded from almost on top of her. Astounded that she had goaded Robert into sending flowers, she followed Sheila's order.

The card simply read: **R.L.**

She didn't even try to guess how he'd known where she worked. After she dodged her co-worker's twenty questions and shooed her out the door, she'd sent him a text.

Mika: Thanks for the flowers they're beautiful! But not to sound picky...
Robert: But yet you're about to be
Mika: Why only 4 flowers? What's up with that?
Robert: Buyers choice

46

When she didn't answer for a full minute he sent another message.

Robert: You'll have to figure it out on your own. You're like a forever unsatisfied spoiled princess
Mika: Whatever and don't call me that
Robert: Sure, whatever the princess wants
Mika: Anyone ever mention that you're an ass?
Robert: At least once a week, it's one of my finest qualities

She'd let him have the last word and enjoyed the rest of the day. Later that week on Wednesday another delivery man showed up. This time to her home late in the evening. The case of wine had arrived! The note with this delivery said: **Enjoy R.L.**

After that Mika hadn't heard from the man. But she sure was enjoying the wine! Since Andrea and Cam had taken her to the party she gave four bottles with them. Reaching her destination, she tried to convince herself that the "contact silence" wasn't why she was stepping into Robert's office building. Mika didn't waste her time checking in with the receptionist. Instead she walked past as if she belonged, and nobody tried to stop her. Looking at the elevator directory she found the floor for the financial advisors, figuring he should be easy to find. However a few people gave her looks as she strolled around his floor.

They were probably curious who the new face was. As she walked by in a bright blue wool coat and an ankle-length purple pencil skirt, which made her the most colorful thing in the office. The building was the epitome of stuffy and sterile. Just being in here was actually giving her the heebie-jeebies. There were a lot of offices on his floor instead of cubicles and that made sense, as talking money was a very private thing. However the exterior walls to the offices were glass, so it was like looking into a fishbowl. Hopefully that would make it easier to hunt for Robert.

Robert heard the commotion a few offices down, before he heard the laugh that told him *trouble* had arrived. He stayed seated and waited. He assumed she would reach him after she was done flirting with the whole office. He had purposely not contacted her, as they were supposed to be sex-only. Plus work needed his focus. However, he'd quickly come to realize Mika was the worst thing to ever happen to his concentration.

Speaking of distractions, *she* finally came into view, walking between Antonio and Eric. The sight of her was like a shot of adrenaline. Seeing her bright, bold and animated between the two men gave him an instant jolt. Antonio was his boy at work, an actual friend. They'd bonded as the only minorities in this division. Plus, he was a cool guy. Antonio gave a quick tap on his door frame, "Hey Robert. It looks like this lovely lady is here to see *you*."

"Unfortunately Antonio, I wasn't aware of the *other* options your company had." Mika gave him a slow smile. "Or I might have been visiting you instead."

"That is indeed a shame." He smiled widely, flirting back. "But you're in good hands with my man Robert here. See you later."

"Thanks Tone." Robert wasn't even looking his way. "Can you close the door on your way out?"

"Sure thing." Antonio closed the door, as Mika took off her coat and sat.

Robert watched silently as she settled in the chair. When she finally sat back, crossing those long legs of hers, he asked, "What are you doing here?"

"I'm not quite sure. Against my better judgement I've taken Andrea's advice. She told me a while back that I should come see you about my money...and here I am."

Ahh, so it wasn't personal. "I see. You should have made an appointment. I can give you thirty to thirty-five minutes, but I have a call coming up."

"Now that I think about it, I don't want you to have all my info. You've already proven to be a prolific stalker." Mika was hoping a joke would lighten his mood. But she forgot who she was dealing with. He didn't blink or crack a smile.

"I'm a complete professional when it comes to my job and my clients' money. But if you want I can recommend a trusted colleague. Maybe Antonio?"

"I don't know him!"

Robert was surprised into a bemused smile at the asinine conversation he was having. "O-kay then, your time is ticking. Do you want to proceed or would you like to leave?"

"Fine, I don't want to hear Andrea's mouth. I'll deal with you. Better the devil you know I guess."

"We'll go through some basic questions, and I can give you a very basic recommendation. If you want to move forward you can set up an official appointment after I send you the paperwork. Does that sound good?"

"Sure, fine." Apparently he wanted to play it completely professional, as if his tongue hadn't been in hard to reach places of her body. Watching him write her name on a notepad, she damned herself for thinking about all the places his *fingers* had been as well.

"What are your investment goals?"

"I would say early retirement, but I actually like what I do. Also I'm big on having funds for travel."

He quirked an eyebrow at her answer but didn't say anything about it. "What type of investor do you see yourself as? Do you prefer low, medium or high-risk investments?"

"I'm okay with high-risk. I mean that's the whole point of this right? No risk, no reward? Besides, if I'm going to take chances I should do it now in life."

Robert wasn't surprised by that answer in the least. She seemed the type that would take risks. Like jumping out of planes and shit for fun. "Okay, so give me a ballpark of what you're working with when it comes to funds to invest."

Mika put a finger on her chin and did some quick mental arithmetic. "Well my base salary is ninety-two thousand as an Associate Creative Director, and we get bonuses from time to time for certain projects. Andrea says I should be investing the full bonus and just pretend like I never got it. I invest five percent into my retirement fund. I know low, so don't lecture me. I can definitely up that to the max. I fool around with a small amount in stocks myself, nothing major. There's my trust fund too. I put that in a basic money market account when I took it over. I think it's about three hundred and twenty-five thousand in there."

Robert dropped his pen and leaned back. "You have three hundred and twenty-five thousand dollars sitting in a basic money market account?" He asked astonished. Both by the amount and the idiocy of her choice.

"Yeah, is that bad? I feel like from your look you think that's bad."

"Jesus woman, no wonder Andrea sent you to me. How long have you been managing it with what amounts to a checking account with low interest?"

"Umm, since I turned twenty-one, so seven years now."

"What a waste. With the right investments, you could easily be at half a million or more by now." He glanced at his watch and saw he needed to wrap this up.

She just shrugged at his proclamation. "Money isn't everything."

Robert scoffed. "This coming from the woman who has more than a quarter-million in savings alone before thirty.

Look, it's clear you could be doing better on all investment fronts. I'll draw up the basic paperwork to get you started with us and email them to you by Monday."

He took out a card and handed it to her. "Call this number after you shoot the forms back to me and Jill will schedule you to come in as soon as I have an opening."

"Okay, that works. Thank you."

Now that business was taken care of, he assessed her. She looked good as usual. Wearing big colorful jewelry that complemented her outfit. A vision of her naked with just the jewelry and maybe some high-heeled boots entered his brain. He got instantly hard and was glad to be sitting down. But it spurred him to ask, "What are you doing next Saturday night?"

"Let me check." Mika went to her phone's calendar. She wasn't trying to be coy or anything, but her weekends were often packed. "The night looks free for now...why?"

"I'm thinking maybe we can get together...do something."

"We'll see."

"Yeah, we will." He gave her a brief smile before frowning. " I'll call you next week."

Knowing when she was being dismissed she stood, putting on her coat. "Don't stress over it...I won't be waiting," she said dryly.

Robert was already half turned to his computer, putting on his headset. "Yeah you will. And text me your personal email so I can send you those papers."

"Surprised you don't have it. You slipping Mr. Stalker," Mika half mumbled as she reached the door.

"I heard that. Women stalk *me*, not the other way around. Shut my door on the way out."

Chapter Eight

Mika had on tight-fitting dark jeans, with a loose off the shoulders cranberry top. Her lips the same shade of red to match. Trying to be cute she had on a coat that was more suited to early fall than the middle of November. She'd kept her jewelry light wearing a simple gold necklace, one semi-gaudy ring and some earrings. The latter a pair of dangling blue and gold stones, meant to contrast with her top.

True to his word Robert had emailed her the investment documents on Monday. Later that week he'd asked if she wanted to catch a movie on Saturday at the Emagine by his house in Royal Oak. After getting over her surprise that they were going anywhere but straight to bed, she'd accepted. He'd even offered to pick her up but she'd declined. She wanted to be able to leave if he was getting on her last nerve, which was a definite possibility with him. They hadn't even picked out a movie yet, Robert only telling her to meet there at six. She was game for whatever so didn't sweat the lack of details.

She saw him standing behind the glass doors as she approached. Robert was looking at his phone so she took the time to assess him. She had to admit he was a fine piece of eye-candy. His wide shoulders filling out the dark-brown, herringbone wool coat he had on. The profile of his face stood sharp and strong, as she watched his full lips part into a rare unguarded smile at something on his screen. Mika had no clue what he had in mind for tonight, but her *lady bits* were hoping it included them. As if he could hear her inner thoughts he looked up, his expression becoming closed off as he opened the door.

"You made it, and on time."

"I said I was coming. I mean I thought about standing you up, but you have the habit of showing up at people's doors." Mika poked.

"Good to see we understand each other."

"Ha, whatever. So what movie do you have in mind?"

"Actually," he said, maneuvering her away from the entrance. "The movie I was thinking of doesn't start until 7:15. I was thinking we could get some dinner first."

"Oh...okay. I don't see why not." First the movie and now dinner, was he trying to soften me up for later? Either way she'd take the food. She followed him to the second floor where the restaurant was housed. He helped her with her coat and seat, before situating himself.

"You looking good," Robert said, across at her.

"Thank you." She almost mentioned that was the first outright compliment he'd ever given her, but thought better of it. Since he was making an effort she decided to tone down her own natural sarcasm.

"I even wore some blue and gold as a peace offering," Mika said pointing at her ears.

That earned her an appreciative smile from Robert before their waitress came over. They both took a quick look at the menu not needing long, they each had eaten here before. They got the garlic cheese bread as a starter, while she ordered a southwest chicken wrap and he got the buffalo one. She tried a fruit beer because the name "Norm's Raggedy Ass" amused her. And once their order was taken, she picked up where they left off.

"You look sharp as well. I can honestly say I never find fault in your style." He nodded his head in thanks. "There is one thing I don't get. Unlike most black men in a conservative corporate role, you don't wear your hair extra short. It doesn't fit the rest of your...disciplined persona."

Smiling widely Robert replied, "It's my way of keeping it real for the culture."

Mika laughed out right, her eyes dancing with delight. "That's what I figured. Like a big 'fuck you' to the man, so to speak. So you *can* be a bit of a rebel huh?"

"If the mood strikes me and the cause is legit. I don't know why you think I'm such a nerd."

"I've never used that word for you. You give off a sophisticated and buttoned-up air, nothing nerdy about that. Besides, nerds can be hot!"

"I feel like there's a *but* coming."

She smiled sheepishly. "But you seem so uptight, which is confusing since you and Cam are so close and he's so chill."

"Certain people make me uptight, mainly you. You seem to have a disruptive effect on my nerves," he said dryly.

"Well, I like it."

Robert shook his head. "You like disrupting my nerves?"

"Sure that too, but I was talking about your hair."

In fact she loved the low curly fade he kept. It was enough for her to grab hold of as they moved together in bed. She liked the fact that he was bold with his natural texture.

"You are a vexing woman. I still don't know if you're ridiculous or interesting."

"Aww, thanks. You are such a sweet-talker. I try my best to stay confounding. Personally, I'd put that trait in the 'interesting' column."

The two grinned at each other across the table as their appetizer and drinks arrived. They spent the rest of the dinner amicably chatting. Robert found out not only was she a football fan but a genuine all around sports watcher. That was unexpected. Now the fact that she was an only child made perfect sense to him. She had a slight spoiled air to her. It was no wonder she naturally grabbed the spotlight wherever she went. She also had no problem with the action movie he'd picked. Turned out it was her favorite genre, comedy coming in a close second.

Now that they both were at a cease fire, he found her sharp and witty. Her sense of humor and sarcasm on par with his even though it was often aimed in his direction. He also confirmed she wasn't shy about eating, which was good. Pretending not to be hungry just because a male was around was stupid. He was finishing off his beer as she started on dessert.

"You seem to have a sweet tooth." He watched her dip a third fry in cinnamon butter.

Mika licked her fingers before answering. She hadn't been able to resist ordering the funnel cake fries. "I know bad habit, but I really love these! Try it! The butter alone is to die for."

Robert tried the dip. "This *is* good."

Her mouth was full, so she just grinned knowingly.

"How do you eat so many sweets and keep your figure? Do you work out a lot?"

"Nope," Mika said with a laugh. "I have a gym membership, and I might go three or four times a month. I guess I just have a high metabolism. At least for now. I love food! It's the reason Thanksgiving is my favorite holiday."

"Really? Well feel free to drop by my place for Thanksgiving dinner next week." As soon as the offer cleared his mouth he wondered where in the hell it had come from? She looked as surprised as he felt.

"Thanks. My family does this up north getaway. We usually go up Wednesday evening. Besides, Cam and Andrea will be at her parents' this year. It would be weird."

"Not really. My cousins and I watch the game, then we eat some turkey. Lots of food to go around." Why did he say that, she'd just given him an out?

"My family will be expecting me, but I appreciate the invite."

Robert let it go, turning the conversation to anything else. He eventually caught their waitress' attention asking for the check. When they left and walked down the stairs Mika made a beeline for the concession stand.

"I want some popcorn," she requested.

"Really? What happened to all that dinner you just ate? That was the whole point of eating first."

"What are you the food police? I like to snack during a movie. Plus I don't come that often and theater popcorn is a treat."

"So you want me to fund your oral fixation to chew?" Robert complained.

"I'll be adding being cheap to the list of your fine qualities. I'll get it myself," she said rolling her eyes.

"Go right ahead. I'm just saying, I can think of other ways for you to work out your oral issues."

Mika couldn't stop the laugh that shot out of her. "You are such a cheap pervert."

Mika bought her popcorn while Robert sprung for another drink for the two of them at the bar. Of course he only made it through half the previews before his hand was in her bucket. She tried to smack him but he got a handful anyway.

"You don't believe in snacking remember. Stay out my stuff."

"Don't be so stingy princess. Didn't anyone ever teach you to share?"

She was surprised the night was going so well, and that they were able to tease and play. She got comfy in the loveseat he'd picked and prepared to enjoy the movie.

When the movie let out around nine-thirty Mika excused herself to use the restroom, Robert said he'd meet her by the front doors. She admitted to being a little nervous to see what came next. Would they go back to his place and get it on? Or would they go their separate ways like two people who were really dating? That last option made her uncomfortable. They were supposed to be just hooking up.

"Get a grip girl. You making this more than it is," she mumbled to herself. "If the man had asked me to come straight to his house, I'd have called him an ass. A dinner and a movie isn't that big of a deal. Friends have dinner...so we're friends with benefits. No biggie."

"Honey are you talking to yourself, or do you need some tissue or something?" The lady from the next stall asked her.

Mika smothered her laugh. "No, sorry, just talking to myself. But thank you!"

"No problem!"

Mika used her feminine wipes just in case she was getting lucky tonight. She was about to find out either way. She made her way out the stall to the sink, before exiting and finding him exactly where he said he would be. She saw more than one group of sista's do a double take as they passed him.

"Are you ready?" She asked coming to stand by him.

"You think *you* ready?"

She saw the look in his eyes, the tone of his voice and knew she would be getting some tonight! "I *stay* ready," she bragged, stepping slightly in front of him.

He looked at her so intensely she almost took a step back. He didn't say anything and for a moment she thought he was going to kiss her then and there. Instead, he just reached past her to open the door.

* * *

It had started to snow as they left but the roads were clear for now. Even so, Robert took his time on the brief drive to his house so she could follow him. He needed time to try for some control anyway. He *had* been about to kiss her right out in the open, he hadn't given a damn about the people walking around them. Which was unlike him. He was a hater of PDA and proud of it. Light and sly sexual touches were okay, sexual banter was always welcome. But blunt displays like kissing in front of a crowd was a firm "no-go" for him.

After the meeting in his office he'd had the urge to get to know her better, outside of the bedroom. In truth he was going to be stuck with her while their friends where married, so they might as well be friendly. On top of that he was intrigued with her personality. How could a highly educated woman be successful, nonchalant and flighty at the same time? He wanted to blame it on her age but they were only three years apart.

Except for her appalling money management she seemed to have the rest of her life together. Owned a home, excelling in her career, and she had a sophisticated yet trendy style going on. He could easily see her living in a city like New York or Cali with the way she carried herself. Mika was a ball of energy, and he had some ideas for how she could put that to use.

Damn but she made him hard! She wasn't afraid to challenge him, to push and poke. Normally that would have turned him off because he could admit to being a controlling bastard at times. Plus he hated games and drama. Instead he found himself playing back, trading barbs and jokes. She didn't seem to be put off or offended by his sometimes acerbic nature.

He pulled up to his house opening the two-car garage, motioning with his arm out the window for her to pull into the second spot. Once they were both in he closed the door and watched as she got out, rubbing her gloved hands against the cold. He'd warm her up soon enough. They entered the back hallway and he led her toward the main part of the house.

"Do you want something to drink? Wine?" He offered.

"No, some water would be good...for after."

"I got you." It turned him on even more to see they were on the *exact* same page on what was about to happen. "Give me your coat. The stairs are right past the den. My bedroom is on the left. There's a connected bathroom if you need it. I'll be up in a few."

She only nodded, walking closer than necessary to hand him her coat. She leaned against him stretching up to give him a light kiss before slowly walking off. She didn't look back to see if he was watching, they both knew he would be. For his part he kept his hands to himself, as he wanted to make sure they made it upstairs. He was too close to the edge to risk putting his hands on her.

He removed something from his outside pocket before hanging up both coats. In the kitchen he retrieved two bottles of cold water before heading to the half-bath on the ground floor. He took his time, then headed back to the kitchen, using the microwave briefly. Removing his sweater and undershirt before loosening his belt, while he waited for the beep. When it was ready, he took the waters in hand and headed up.

Apparently they were still on the same wavelength because he found her stretched out lazily on his king-sized bed, only in her bra and panties. She'd even taken her necklace and ring off. He appreciated that the U of M colored earrings still hung from her ears. He sat everything in his hands down on the dresser.

"You might as well take the rest off."

"So now you lazy too? What would that leave you to do?" Mika sat up, but otherwise didn't comply with his suggestion.

He just stared at her, sliding off his pants and underwear, her eyes following his every move. "Come here...I got something for you."

She laughed lightly, amused. "I *bet* you do. What else you got over there *besides* water that I actually want?"

"Dessert."

That piqued her interest and she slowly got up and walked over to him, stopping just out of reach. "Weren't you telling me I ate too much a while ago?" She reached behind her back unhooking her bra, letting the material catch on her nipples as it fell down her arms. "I thought I was supposed to be working off some of those calories."

He was transfixed, watching her swaying breasts as she removed her panties. The vixen bent forward unnecessarily to take them off, one foot at a time. He fisted his dick and begin to slowly stroke it.

Finding his voice, he said, "You can eat *and* have sex with this." He reached behind him picking up the small cup before closing the distance between them. Dipping his fingers in the warm cinnamon butter he'd gotten from the restaurant, he spread some on each nipple.

Delighted she laughed, which quickly turned into a choked moan of pleasure as he lowered his head to slowly and thoroughly suck the concoction from each breast.

"Damn, that's good."

"Gimme some. *I'm* the one with a sweet tooth." She took his mouth in a slow, deep kiss, sucking the sweetness from him.

It was a while before she dipped her fingers in the cup, getting a good amount before painting the spread on his chest and stomach. Wrapping her slick hand around him she stroked him up and down. When a deep groan came from his throat, she backed him up to the dresser taking the cup and sitting it down. She licked his nipples—her hand still working—before following the trail with her mouth until she had to sink to her knees. Looking up she saw his eyes were half-closed and clouded with arousal.

She licked her lips and said, "You know how I love my sweets." Before taking him in her mouth.

The playful date officially flowed into playful sex. Between laughs, and exploratory touches they took turns satisfying their cravings before she found herself straddling him. He handed her a condom and she smiled in thanks before she put it on him. Lowering herself down on his rigid length she begin to ride him. Alternating between fast and slow, shallow and deep strokes. His hands doing the same to her breasts, gentle then rough as they squeezed, shaped and pinched her nipples. Robert also used his hands to guide her hips, smack her ass and strum her clit when he was ready for her to cum.

After a water break, they went on to have sex two more times. She lay half on his chest as their breathing got back to normal.

"I should probably head out," she ventured. Not moving a muscle, except for her finger lightly flicking one of his nipples.

Robert didn't bother opening his eyes as he answered, nor did he remove his arm from around her. "If you really want to go out in the snow after midnight, feel free. If you staying...stop playing with my nipple so I can sleep."

Instead of leaving his nipple alone, she pinched it and got a firm slap on her ass for her trouble. Neither spoke as she snuggled next to him and closed her eyes. She had no desire to go out in the wet snow when she had a nice, warm body to lay next to.

Chapter Nine

Mika wrapped up her work on Thanksgiving near noon, having been at it since eight in the morning. Saving, she sent updates where needed and was finally off the clock! The rushed redesign and changes had come in late Wednesday after work, right as she had been loading up her car to head out. She damned herself for even picking up the phone. Her boss made it clear he considered this a rare emergency. The conversation when she had called her mother to explain however hadn't gone well.

"This is unacceptable Mikala. It's the holiday for goodness sake! Your boss knows you always go out of town."

"I know Mother. But that's why I can't blow off this assignment. Every year I'm gone. This year I volunteered to be on call. Honestly we've never had a crisis on the holiday so I didn't' think much of it. But surprise I'm up!"

"Just tell them you already left. Let someone else do it."

"I can't do that. I have a responsibility to the team."

"But this is family time!"

"They have a family and a life too!" Mika raised her tone as well only to be met with silence. Sighing she continued. *"Look, the sooner I stop arguing with you and get off the phone, the sooner I can get this done. Depending on how much is needed I may make it tomorrow for Thanksgiving. If not I promise I'll drive up early Friday and still be able to spend the weekend with everyone...okay?"*

"Fine," her mother said stiffly.

"Bye Mother."

Now looking out the window in her home office, she watched the lightly falling snow and considered her options. If she left soon she could make the trip before it got completely dark. However it had snowed late last night, and up north normally got more than her area which meant the roads were probably a mess. She shook her head and decided it wasn't worth it. The forecast called for on and off again snow flurries until late tonight. Firm on her decision she sent her mother a brief text, letting her know she'd be up by noon on Friday. Turning off her ringer she headed for a shower.

Finished, she felt refreshed and got dressed in a comfy football outfit so she could settle in to cheer on her poor but determined Lions. It was odd, for as much as she hated her family trips to the cabin she was feeling a little lonely. She enjoyed watching the game with her father and uncle. While her cousins, mother and aunt actually left them alone for a few hours.

She hadn't always enjoyed sports, but she'd learned at an early age it was one way she could spend time with her father. Daddy had been so busy when she was younger, constantly having to prove he deserved his position. He got paid tons of money, and he definitely earned *every* penny of it. She had grown to love sports after a while. She couldn't even go crash at Andrea and Cam's place, as they were spending this holiday with Andrea's parents. Making a snap decision, she grabbed up her purse and phone before putting on some shoes with a matching coat before heading out the door.

* * *

She didn't allow herself to think about her destination as she drove, figuring it would all work out in the end. If push came to shove there were some nice restaurants out this way, if she ended up needing to grab some turkey. She had almost forgotten about Robert's hastily given invitation. It had been clear he regretted the words which was another reason she'd been surprised to receive flowers again this Monday at work.

This time there had been three, an orange rose, a yellow rose and a blue hyacinth. She was still clueless on why the odd number and pairings. This batch had been less than the first one. Was this some kind of countdown? She had finally stopped trying to figure out the workings of a man like Robert's brain and just enjoyed the flowers. Now she was on her way to crash his family's Thanksgiving dinner.

Sitting in his driveway for a few moments, she counseled herself to get a grip. She braved her way to the front door and rang the doorbell, putting on her most charming smile. She blinked at the pretty shortish woman who opened the door, looking her up and down.

"Yes? Can I help you?"

"Hi, I'm a guest of Robert's." She didn't wait for an invitation as she angled her body inside the door.

Brihanna was so taken aback by the pronouncement that she didn't think to block her. The smiling woman stood in her brother's hall already taking off her coat.

"You say you're a friend of Roberts?" Brihanna asked, crossing her arms as she watched the woman put her coat in a hall closet. It was obvious she knew her way around.

"I wouldn't go that far. We're acquaintances. I'm Andrea's best friend Mika. I know him through her and Cam."

"Oh! That's right! I thought you looked familiar!" Brihanna exclaimed. "I recognize you from the wedding video."

"Yep, that was me."

"Nice to meet you. I'm Brihanna! I don't know why my blockheaded brother didn't mention you were coming." Brihanna started walking away and gestured for Mika to follow.

Mika started to correct her, but now she was the one being steamrolled as Robert's sister quickly ushered her into his beautiful kitchen. The two women cooking stopped what they were doing and turned to look at the newcomer, both of their faces showing mild curiosity.

"Who is this?"

"Aunt Dolores, really?"

"I'm Andrea's best friend, Mika Harrison," Mika spoke up, deciding to lead with the association that made a difference.

"Mama remember? She was in the wedding," Brihanna clarified.

Mika watched the women's faces stretch into pleased smiles.

"Ahh, yes! It was such a beautiful wedding. You all looked wonderful. We were so happy sweet Andrea finally settled down with our Cam!" The woman speaking moved forward and embraced Mika in a hug before she could protest.

"I'm Johanna, Robert and Brihanna's mother. Welcome!" Pulling back, she gestured to the other woman holding a spoon. "That's my sister Dolores."

Mika preempted a hug by reaching her hand. "It's nice to meet you all. Andrea told me a lot about you guys from her visit last year. She really enjoyed it."

The older women were beaming with pleasure at that comment, when Robert walked in.

"Who was at the door?" He stopped in his tracks when he caught sight of her. "What are you doing here?"

Mika's smile slipped a bit, his tone definitely didn't seem pleased. His facial expression wasn't much better. "You invited me. I know you're getting old, but I didn't think your memory was gone yet." The whole kitchen—sizzling pots included, seemed to hold its collective breath waiting on his response.

Robert, who still hadn't glanced at his family stepped closer. Mika stood in his kitchen giving him attitude, looking sexy yet casual at the same time. She was holding a Traders Joe's bag as she calmly waited on his response.

"You told me you'd be out of town."

"Plans changed," she said.

As he hiked a brow and crossed his arms, she let out a huff of her own. Annoyed at having to explain herself.

"I got stuck redoing a major project for work yesterday. I just finished a little while ago, so I'm driving up tomorrow instead. Which is why I thought I'd take you up on your invite...if that's okay?" She asked the last with hesitation.

"No its fine, just unexpected," Robert said softly. He was about to close the space between them when the sound of a throat clearing caught his attention. His mother was giving him a look. He really *had* forgotten the other people in the room. "I'm sorry. Let me introduce you to everyone."

"Already taken care of," Dolores said tersely, her own eyes narrowed on her only nephew.

"Of course Mika is welcome. Any friend of Cam's is. What's that in your hand honey?" Johanna reached out and took the bag.

"Just my small contribution. Sorry, I didn't bring a dish."

"Can you cook?" Dolores asked her customary question as she moved her sister out the way to peer inside the bag.

"No ma'am, pretty much not a lick!" Mika said cheerfully, her smile back in place. "Not unless you guys want breakfast for dinner."

"Don't nobody want eggs on Thanksgiving day," Dolores said, rolling her eyes. "Get on with you then. Go and watch your football game."

Mika looked down at the time on her phone. She had only missed about five minutes of the game. Turning back to Robert she asked, "Did anyone score yet?"

Before he could answer Brihanna interrupted. "Hey...why does she get out of kitchen duty and I don't?"

"One, because she's a guest." Johanna shook her head at her youngest.

"Two," Dolores chimed in. "*You* need to learn to cook. We're trying to prepare you for the day you get a man. You know, that day *way in the future,* so you can cook for your husband."

"Why do you have to say it like that!" Brihanna snapped at her aunt.

At the same time her mother interjected, "I've told you about messing with my baby."

"Your baby not gone ever have no babies, if she don't learn how to cook! Or if she does they gone all starve."

As a full-out argument started Mika backed away from the women and ran into Robert. "I'll just...get out the way....umm I'll...check in later."

All three women waved her away, not even glancing at her as they continued the family squabble. Robert took her arm leading her from the kitchen.

"You leaving your sister like that?" She whispered to him.

"I'm not getting into the middle of that old argument. Besides, my sister is tough, she can take care of herself."

Chapter Ten

Robert watched the surprise on all his cousins' faces as Mika walked into the room and went straight for Devon and Darrell. Those two were surprised but pleased to see her. He took the time to introduce her to the other members of his family in the room. She took the introductions in stride and then settled down in the armchair Thomas offered her. At least she wouldn't be sitting between his two perpetually horny relatives this time.

Everyone else turned back to the game while he tried to process her presence. He hadn't expected to see her today, nevertheless here she was. He tried to remind himself it wasn't that big of a deal. Since he'd been hosting the holiday for the last eight years, he had invited at least three women to break bread. The same could be said for his unattached cousins. Well Devon and Darrell certainly had a time or two, though Thomas tended to keep whatever relationships he had more private. Robert just didn't want any of his family getting the wrong idea.

The game went by in a blur. People in and out, voices raised, kids being kids. The Lions gave it a good effort, but lost it in the last two minutes. No one was really surprised. Everyone was familiar with the hope/disgust combo of emotions that went along with being a Lions fan. They had been talking about all the mistakes that were made when his mother stuck her head around the corner.

"Mika, can you give us a hand in the kitchen?"

"I sure can. I'm ready to eat my sorrows away with food."

Robert watched as she hopped up from her seat.

"Thank you." Johanna turned to the rest of them. "We should be ready to eat in a few."

Edward sent the kids and teens to wash up, then turned to grin at Robert. "So...what's up with Mika? She a *special* friend of yours?"

"What? No, I told you how I know her through Cam's wife."

"Good, because I'm thinking of making her a *special* friend of mine," Devon pronounced.

"Sorry my brother, I think I got this one on lock. I can tell she's feeling me. We vibing," Darrell boasted.

"Neither one of you..." Robert waved his hand dismissively in their direction. "Would get anywhere with her."

Thomas looked confused. "Why you say that? She got a man?"

"No."

Devon smiled, "Well then, I'll take my shot and see what happens. Might be destiny. I have met her twice now in your house."

"Look, she's a friend of a friend and a guest in my house. I don't want ya'll harassing her."

Luckily his aunt chose that moment to announce dinner was served. Robert was glad to stop the conversation and took the time to do a brief errand outside, before washing his hands. Coming in the dining room he found Mika once again sitting between the family members he wanted her to stay away from.

He stood on the other side of the table and asked, "Is that where you're going to sit?"

"It's where I sat...so yes."

As the two continued to stare each other down, Johanna lightly rapped her hand on the table to get her son's attention. "Let's *all* sit down and say this prayer, so we can eat. Robert why don't you lead us this year."

That request took all the family members by surprise, including Robert. Usually Dolores or Thomas led the benediction. It got him seated however, and after a brief prayer they went on to have dinner.

As usual, after dinner the adult males of the house retired to the patio for a drink or two and a little private time to chill. The guys got settled, as Robert pulled out the retractable awning, since light snow was falling. The men had barely taken their first few sips before the door opened to reveal Mika walking out with a shot glass.

"Hey scoot over," she said to Robert, squeezing herself into the oversized deck chair. It was made for a big man, but not two people. The rest of the men had their mouths open, while her host just looked at her exasperated.

"Why are you out here with no coat?"

"What? It's not that cold, otherwise it couldn't snow. Anyway I saw you had the awning. Figured I'd run out and get a couple of shots. Then I'll get out of your way."

"Mika, I can keep you warm. Come on over here." Darrell patted his lap.

"Oh I have no doubt you can." Mika gave him a wink while Devon was pouring her a shot. "But I'm comfy right here. Besides, Robert will give me his coat."

"The hell I will. Why would I do that when you *chose* to come out without one?"

"Didn't we talk about this before? You're supposed to be courteous to your guest and see to their needs. Put their comfort above your own," she chastised him before downing her shot.

"And didn't I tell you then, my house my way. Besides, you said you're leaving after a couple of shots. You've had one. Devon pour her another, so she can go and stop hogging my seat."

"Maybe I'll go, maybe I won't." But she held out her glass anyway.

His two older cousins hadn't picked their jaws all the way up yet, while the younger two were grinning at her and shaking their heads.

"You could give me the chair you know."

"Not happening." Robert purposely went into a man-spread with his legs forcing her even more into the corner.

"Ugh, you suck." She scooted forward sitting on the very edge, drinking half her latest shot before turning a bright smile on the rest of the men. "So, what are you guys talking about? Was it me and if so, was it anything good?"

Edward finally laughed outright. "No, but it will be whenever you go in the house."

She gave him a grin back. "That's fair enough."

"Exactly *when* will you be exiting this patio?" Robert questioned, shooting her a pointed look.

Mika slowly finished her drink before saying. "I guess *now*, since you're rude and won't loan me your coat." She stood up. "Just so you know, I'm adding stingy to the list."

"You do that." He shifted getting comfortable.

"It's done." She moved off towards the door, leaving as quickly as she'd come.

There was a prolonged moment of silence before everyone but Robert burst out laughing.

"Man what was that! The Mika and Robert show?" Thomas asked still laughing.

"Naw, she's her own headliner," Robert said with a small smile.

"Got *that* right. She can command *my* attention anytime." Darrell exclaimed.

The others laughed, but Robert scowled before saying, "She's out of your league little cus."

"Says who? She seems just right to me, we're even the same age."

Robert scoffed loudly. "She'd eat you alive."

"Hell that's an asset to him, not a detriment," Devon joked. "Though I agree. She's more my speed, I know just what to do with her." A thoughtful leer on his face as he looked toward the house.

Robert hardened his voice. "Neither of you will have the chance to fail. She's off limits."

Silence. The two younger men shared a look before looking at their older brothers.

Edward shifted in his chair before he stated, "So you two *are* a thing?"

"No," Robert answered shortly. He didn't know why he didn't tell them she was his current playmate, but he just thought it was none of their damn business.

"You sure?" Devon snapped. "Cause this is the second time today you've warned us off her." And Devon didn't appreciate it either.

"It wasn't a warning...it was a statement. You can flirt all you want but don't try anything serious with her."

"Not that I'm technically interested mind you, bit young for me though she's certainly nice looking. Why are you being so territorial if you've got no claim to her?" Thomas pointed out trying to get Robert to be reasonable.

"Cam thinks of her as a little sister...his words. I just think it would be a bad idea for any of us to get involved with her."

The brothers all looked at each other. That truly was a flimsy excuse and they all knew it.

Edward couldn't take it. "I'm calling bullshit." He wasn't that concerned about Robert's temper.

"Call it what you want, that's the way it is."

"Umm, bullshit!" Darrell gave a loud cough over the word. "So that's why you can't keep your eyes off her either huh? Guess we not the only ones panting after her."

"I never said she wasn't fine."

"At least that's *one* lie you not telling yourself," Darrell mumbled.

"What did you say?"

"Nothing cus, nothing." Darrell didn't feel like arguing. Mika was fine and he'd hit it if he could. But she wasn't worth going head to head with Robert, just because she was cool and fun to be around.

"Good, let's just drop it." Robert took a big gulp of his drink. He was tired of talking about this.

Apparently Devon wasn't. "Naw, that's some messed up shit, and you know it. If you want her man up and make it known. But don't cock-block."

Robert leaned forward in his chair like he was about to get up.

"Hey!" Thomas slashed his hand in the air, bringing a halt to the brewing confrontation. He trained his focus on Robert. "Look man, I don't know what is or isn't going on with you two. And frankly, it's really none of our business. But she's a grown woman and not blood-related to any of us. You can't go around telling other men to back off without expecting them to think you've got designs on her."

"She's not a fucking set of luggage," Robert said through clenched teeth as he *still* stared down Devon.

"Exactly. She's a gorgeous, engaging and vibrant woman, who also loves sports. If you really have no interest in her that's cool," Edward spoke up, deciding to be real blunt. "But other men will. Don't get mad when someone else reaches out, and she gives them what you won't take."

Standing up Robert prepared to go inside, he'd had enough. His mother would kill him if he knocked one—or several—of his cousins out. "I'm done. I've told ya'll it's not that deep."

As Robert went inside Thomas shook his head. "I'm calling bullshit too."

Robert went through the house and veered towards the kitchen, finding his aunt putting up the food.

"Aunt D, where's Mika?"

"You all right?" When he didn't say anything, she turned back to her task. "Okay whatever. Your friend was getting ready to go. I just handed her a plate not long ago."

"Really? Okay thanks."

"Mmm-hmm." Delores didn't say anything else as she watched him rush out the kitchen. Her nephew had one hard head. It was clear to her he was in the process of getting it cracked *wide* open.

Robert found Mika in the front hall zipping up her coat and talking to Brihanna, a to-go bag dangling from her hand. Walking right in-between them he butted in. "You were just going to leave without telling me?"

Mika rolled her eyes. "I figured since you were a rude host, I'd be a rude guest."

"Yes rude, didn't you see me talking here?" Brihanna complained.

Robert gave her the universal thumb jerk to take a hike.

"What is your problem?" Brihanna asked before turning back to Mika. "Anyway, it was good to meet you. Keep in touch."

Mika gave her a genuine smile. "Will do. You, me and Andrea will have to do lunch sometime."

"Sounds good!" Brihanna gave her brother a nudge with her shoulder as she brushed past him.

Alone Mika frowned at Robert, who was looking more irritable than normal. "You okay?"

"Yeah, yeah. Just annoyed you were going to sneak off."

"I wasn't sneaking. I said goodbye to your mom and everyone else inside the house. You were outside in your boys' club. Besides it's almost seven-thirty, I'm tired." She proved it when a huge yawn took over. "I've been working hard on that project since Wednesday night until right before I came here. I need to crash, so I can head out early in the morning."

"My bad, I forgot about that. Let me walk you out."

"Okay." When she went to go out the front door, he steered her down the hall toward the garage entrance.

"Why are we going this way, I parked out front."

"I moved your car right before dinner. Figured you wouldn't have to clean it off when you left."

"That was really nice. You do know I'll have to add thief to your list though."

"You're welcome, and what are you talking about?" They had reached the garage and Robert pressed the button, so the door would lift.

"You took my keys and moved my car without permission. I call that thievery."

"See, no good deed goes unpunished."

"Nope. Thanks for allowing me to crash your holiday." She offered a soft smile. "I enjoyed your family and dinner. Make sure to tell your cousins I said bye."

"Yeah." He muttered at the mention of them. "It's no big deal, we often have miscellaneous people over for the holidays. "

"Oh." Mika was taken aback by the comment. "Well in that case, thanks for giving this stray a warm place and a meal for the day."

Robert had seen the flash of hurt in her eyes before she'd covered it with sarcasm. Damnit, he hadn't meant it to sound that way. He seemed to be constantly putting his foot in his mouth today.

"I didn't mean it like—" he started.

"I know. No biggie, honestly. I gotta go. Mika got in her car itching to leave.

"Well let me know when you get home. The roads might be bad with this slush."

"Mmm...okay." She shut the door abruptly, buckled up and gave him a distracted wave as she backed out and left.

Chapter Eleven

Robert was surprised Cam had hit him up today about hanging out. It was a week after Thanksgiving and they were meeting at Hopcat for a few drinks. He'd seen Mika on Wednesday for her appointment at his office. In his mind it had been a "cool" meeting. She'd been all business, bringing the necessary paperwork for them to go over that he'd emailed her about. She hadn't cracked a joke at his expense, not even once.

At first he figured she was focusing on the business of her money, like any sane person would. But she seemed just a tad stiff, no real sparkle or challenge in her eyes. She seemed subdued and that was a word he didn't equate with her. He shook off his thoughts as the waitress set both meals down. Cam had texted he was running late and told Robert to order for him. The timing seemed to be good, as he saw his friend heading his way.

"My bad man. Andrea's going out tonight. I needed to remind her of what she has at home, if you get my drift."

Robert couldn't stop the laugh that came out. "What! Hasn't she gone out with her girls since the wedding?"

"Yeah, but this is different. Tonight's Mika's birthday. I don't know what they have planned and didn't ask. Figured it was better not to know."

"Huh, her birthday is November 30th. Doesn't that makes her a Sagittarius?"

"Yeah, I guess," Cam said around a mouthful of his hamburger.

"Hmm." Robert dug into his own food. Cam had done the right thing by laying it on his wife before she partied. There was no telling what Mika might have planned.

* * *

Mika was be getting old. She was officially twenty-nine, and she didn't know if she liked it. Her *body* sure didn't as she laid on her couch Sunday, dead tired. The start of her birthday weekend kicked off on Friday, with a little club hopping with work friends. On Saturday she'd invited her close girlfriends, a handful of associates and even her cousins out.

The crew of fifteen had headed to Niki's first, getting warmed up with food, drinks, and dancing for a few hours. She'd copped some front-row seats for a concert at Sound Board in Motor City Casino, so they headed there next. Afterwards she gave everyone a $100 bill, so they could play the slots. Robert would skin her alive if he knew she'd paid for a Hummer limo, group concert tickets *and* gave out cash to celebrate her birthday. Thankfully, he would never find out.

Right now she didn't want to think about him. Normally she would have been planning a brief trip to celebrate her born-day on top of the partying. With Robert's dire warnings about overspending ringing in her ears, she'd opted out this year. Besides, her body was betraying her before thirty. Which is why she found herself feeling sleepy and it was barely five-thirty in the afternoon. She was seriously thinking about going into her bedroom for an official nap, when her phone signaled a text.

Robert: I'm in the mood...you game?

Mika looked at her phone for a few seconds before flopping back onto her couch. *Was* she game? Besides being tired she wasn't sure she wanted to continue the arrangement they had. There was no denying he was fantastic in bed. To be honest she had assumed the Vegas hook-up had been super good due to their drunkenness. You know when you're *very* drunk, day old pizza and cold fries might taste like the best meal of your life. She'd figured it was the same with sex. Instead she found him to be inventive, responsive and most of all attentive to her needs between the sheets.

Which was a total 180, to how she'd first pegged him on that airplane. She would have expected an uptight, "I'm always right and better than you" guy to be just as stiff and uncompromising in bed. No the sex wasn't the problem, it was everything else. She was starting to think it might be better to find another stallion for her stable. Glancing at the phone, she saw that he hadn't added anything. He wasn't the type of man to beg or even ask twice. Letting out a huge sigh she got prepared to respond. Why should she deny herself birthday sex?

Mika: I'm game...what you got in mind?
Robert: Meet me at my place at 7
Mika: You come out this way, it's my birthday weekend
Robert: Yeah I might have heard something about that
Robert: But you need to come out here for what I got in mind

"What the hell?" This is why she should leave his arrogant ass alone. And she would...as soon as she got this last taste.

Mika: Fine but this better be worth my time and drive
Robert: It always is

She didn't bother responding to his boast. She would take a thirty minute nap to get her nerves right before going to deal with him.

Mika overslept, or at least that's the story she was sticking to. She was pretty sure her subconscious was being petty. Which was also why instead of wearing something sexy, she'd put on jeans and a sweatshirt and for once she was wearing sneakers as well.

She couldn't bring herself to go completely "plain Jane", so she was still wearing a sexy set of underwear. Mika threw her hair in a high bushy ponytail and called it a day. Even with minimum fanfare she didn't make it to his house until 7:15.

She had barely rang the doorbell before he opened up, stepped out and closed it. "What—?"

"Come on you're late." He propelled her back down the steps towards his Lincoln. "We'll be late if we waste any more time."

He had bundled her inside before she found her voice. "Wait just a minute, I thought we were hooking up. I drove all the way out here expecting some birthday get-down. Not an abduction."

He actually rolled his eyes at her last comment. "I never said you were coming here for sex, though I have zero problem giving you some before the night is out. Right now, we have someplace to be." Starting the car, he drove out his neighborhood.

"You said you were in the *mood*."

"Right, but I never said for what. Not *my* fault your brain is preoccupied with sex."

"I'm not! You implied—" Mika cut herself off.

She knew it was a little ridiculous to be upset that he hadn't accosted her in the driveway. But she was tired of the mixed messages he was sending. He had been the one to set the rules in the first place, yet he tended to switch them up whenever he felt like it. He wasn't treating her like a mere booty-call, and most women would have been thrilled with that. *She* wasn't most women and didn't appreciate these blurred lines. This was *not* the way she had intended to end her birthday weekend.

She took a couple of breaths and finally spit out, "Well lead on, mighty *Lorde* of adventure."

Robert didn't say anything, just continued to drive. His mind was frantically trying to figure out what he'd done wrong in the three minutes they'd been together. When a woman had to cut herself off mid-sentence it was because she was trying to keep from going *all* the way off. Further she made it clear she didn't want to talk by turning up the radio. Fine with him. Shit, if her attitude didn't change this was going to be a long night.

Mika cracked her eyes open as she felt the car stop. Her quick meditation had helped. She was feeling calmer now. She would make the best of it. Though she wasn't above demanding to be taken home or even calling an Uber if need be. Plenty of men had been fooled into taking her easygoing ways for weakness. Looking around, she could tell they were in a parking structure.

"Where are we?"

"At the Detroit Zoo," Robert answered getting out.

It was barely over 50 degrees and already full dark. "What are we doing here?"

Robert considered what he should say as he studied her. In the end he didn't smile or explain. He simply held out his hand and said, "Trust me...and you'll find out."

She didn't smile either. Instead she looked at his hand, then back to his face. God help her but that was the problem. She *did* trust him, even though she knew she shouldn't. Stepping forward she took his hand. "Okay Mr. Kidnapper...show me what you got."

* * *

Mika couldn't believe they were at the Zoo. The knowledge immediately put her in a better mood. She was an animal lover from afar. Her parents had never let her have a pet. They were convinced she wouldn't be responsible, and neither parent had time to take care of a pet. She'd thought about getting a dog or cat once she'd had her own home. Sad to say as an adult she didn't think she had time now either.

She'd never been to the zoo at night. The last time she'd visited had been in high school. As they stood in line for tickets, she turned to him with a real smile.

"What is this?"

"It's called Wild Lights. The zoo has it every year. They do elaborate light displays throughout half the place for a month or so." Robert felt his shoulders relax, seemed like the crisis had been averted.

"How cool! Have you been before?"

"No, I only know about it because it's hard to miss the lights each year on my drive home."

"Well I'm looking forward to it! It's been at least a decade since I've been to the Zoo." She was bouncing on her toes, actually glad to have on some kicks. They walked through the gates and immediately saw the word "welcome" in holiday-colored lights, with a field of lighted reindeer behind the sign.

"Oooh, I want a picture!"

Shoving her phone in his hand, she ran over to the sign while he took the shot. They continued on looking at displays of colorful birds in flight, and staged displays of elephants and penguins all lighting the walking path. About ten minutes in they came to a snack hut.

"It's cold, let's get something hot to drink," Robert steered her over to the line.

"They have spiked hot cocoa. I'll take that!"

"They have funnel cake fries, you sure you don't want those too?" Robert teased.

Looking up at him she actually felt herself blush as the memories hit her. Hopefully he'd think it was from the cold. "I saw. Maybe on the way back. They only have frosting for the dip anyway. Nothing as good as what we had."

When they made it to the window he ordered two spiked hot chocolates, paying extra for the keepsake mugs as well. They were both grateful to have the hot liquid as it helped beat off the cold. She put her arm through his and snuggled against his side. Only to share warmth...is what she told herself. Walking on they saw a sleigh arched in the air as if it were flying, then came upon a small ice rink. They passed on actually skating, only pausing there for a while to talk and watch the others fall on the ice. From there they came to the restaurant and decided to grab some pizza while finishing their drinks.

Mika was having a great time. She loved doing new things, and she couldn't believe she'd never been here before. Then again there was always so much going on in and around the Metro Detroit area. She'd have to thank him for the evening. It was sweet. She would assume it was for her birthday weekend. Even so, he had no obligation to acknowledge or do anything to celebrate her day. She was touched by his thoughtfulness. After eating they made the loop back on the other side of the path and came across the theater.

"Hey, they're playing Rudolph! Let's go in."

"Really?" Robert said doubtfully. "You really want to see that?"

"Yeah why not! Everyone likes an underdog. Plus come on, don't you want to sing Rudolph the Red Nose Reindeer?"

"Umm, no."

She pulled him inside anyway pointing to a sign. "And see it's free, you can't have a problem with free. Free 4D showing."

"You got me, I never argue with free."

They stood in line chatting during the short wait for the next show. It was after nine o'clock, so mostly it was only adults with a few older kids here and there. Once inside the small theater, with their 4D glasses on they settled in to enjoy the fifteen-minute show. To say she wasn't ready when fake snow started to fall on her head was an understatement, along with the piped-in smell of peppermint. She was enjoying the abridged version of the childhood movie. Until during the chase scene with the cranky snow monster Bumble, slush splashed on screen and water squirted up into the audience's faces.

"Okay, they taking this 4D thing too far. I don't know where that water's been!"

Robert laughed at her, wiping his own face. "Hey, they just keeping it real."

"*Too real*," she mumbled before focusing on the final minutes of the movie.

True to his word he refused to sing the song at the end. Leaving they were funneled into a two-room gallery filled with various nature photos. They took a few minutes to look around which helped her forget the assault from the show.

"You ready to go?"

"Yeah." The crowd leaving had to contend with the crowd coming in, and he held her hand while navigating them out. She didn't object when the hand-holding continued even once they were back outside. As they headed back towards the entrance they came across a huge lighted lion.

"I want a picture next to this."

"Okay, hand me your phone."

"Take this one with me." Mika persisted.

"I'm not huge on taking pictures."

"Don't spoil my night." She turned around and called out to the first person who made eye contact. Which happened to be an older couple.

"I'm sorry to bother you. Would you mind taking a quick picture of the two of us?"

"Not at all," the lady said taking Mika's phone.

Robert didn't protest further and even smiled for the shot.

"Thank you!" Mika waved the nice couple off.

"Let me see it." Robert reached for the phone.

"No, you said you didn't want to take it."

They argued and wrestled over the phone laughing as they continued on. Not long after they were back in the parking structure getting into his car. As they buckled up she turned to face him.

"Hey thanks for tonight. It was a really fun surprise. I'm sorry about earlier. I didn't know what was going on."

"Yeah that would be my fault. I didn't mention we needed to be somewhere by 7:30, which is why I was rushing when you arrived. I could have given you a heads up. Anyway, I'm glad you enjoyed the evening."

"I did enjoy it! What about you?"

"It was cool. I need to bring my little cousins here next year. You think they'll like it?"

"I don't see why not. So what's on the agenda next?"

"My place," Robert said starting the car. "I'm thinking we should both call off work tomorrow."

Mika burst out laughing, "What? You can't be serious."

"Why not? You asked what I had planned. I see a *long* night for both of us, and it won't be spent sleeping."

"Even so you assume it's going to be *call off work* worthy?"

"Oh I know so. I guarantee it."

Chapter Twelve

As the second week of December came to a close Robert was already tired of cold weather. While he was accustomed to it like any other Michigander, it didn't mean he had to *like* it. The first real snow of the season had come a week ago, dumping six inches overnight. Even a week later three inches still remained on the ground. This was definitely "cuddle-buddy" weather. He supposed Mika was his as he hadn't had sex with anyone else since August.

They'd spent the night after the zoo getting down twice before passing out for the night. He had originally been joking about calling off work. That was before she'd woken him up with a blowjob, followed with a slow ride. He'd barely had enough energy to call his office. Robert hadn't skipped work for a woman since his college days of work-study.

She had showed off her only cooking skills by making him a hearty breakfast, which had actually been delicious. From there it was a morning and afternoon spent watching movies and talking. A specific portion of their conversation stuck out in his mind.

They were lounging on the couch with Mika wearing her sweatshirt and a pair of his boxers, as she laid crossways in his lap. She didn't seem to get the concept of personal space. He had suddenly looked down at her and stated, "You are so not my type."

"Oh? You mean, intelligent, beautiful, and creative? I agree, that isn't your type."

"No, I meant light-skinned."

Mika sat up so she could face him.

"Don't tell me you're one of those brothers who's got color issues. Like you never date light-skin women?"

"No, I'm not. I've dated and been with women of your complexion several times. But they are just not my first preference."

"Oh really...and why is that?"

He watched her slowly cross her arms and knew she was ready for a fight. "Because I feel like they're all out for the same thing. Seems like they find the blackest brother they can date to validate their blackness. They also seem to be high-maintenance more often than not."

He was preparing for the worst when she burst out laughing instead.

"Really Robert? That is such old and tired crap. It's like saying you're sleeping with me to get as close as you can to being with a white woman. Is that true?"

"Hell no!"

"You sure? Many darker men put a lighter woman on their arm, or marry them as a trophy wife. Like a badge of honor all successful black men need to show they made it."

"That's not always—"

She cut him off. "It is more often than not. All you gotta do is glance at the top actors, sport stars, etc."

He went to speak again and she waved him quiet. "And I've dated men of all races. I appreciate handsome men of all ethnicities, but I seem to be most attracted to black men...of all hues. Speaking just for myself, I don't need anything about myself 'validated'. Are we clear on that?"

"Sure thing princess." He tried playing with her loose curls.

"Don't try to distract me." She batted his hand away. "Besides, you are definitely not my type either."

"I'm every woman's type." He pulled her back across his lap before she could resist.

"Nope, not mine. I don't like stuck-up, stiff, know it all's."

He ran his hand up over her breast. "I'm not stuck-up, I have standards. Also I do know best, it's been proven." She snorted and pinched his side. *"And I only have one thing that's stiff, and you seem to really enjoy it."*

That had ended any talking about that subject, starting a make out session instead.

Now he was leaving the gym a little after one on Saturday. The truth was he was already feeling bored at the prospect of heading home. He wondered what Mika was up to? He dialed her from the car.

"Hey, what you doing?" he asked when she answered.

"Nothing. Why?"

"I just finished working out downtown. Thought maybe I could stop by."

"Oh...sorry, but today's not good. I'm not in the mood for company, feeling a little tired."

Robert had noticed she sounded off. "Everything alright?"

"Yeah, just been a long week. I might watch some screen, probably take a nap. Sorry."

"Do you need anything?"

"Nope, just rest." And to get off this phone she thought.

"Okay, I'll talk to you later."

Mika said goodbye and exhaled. She hadn't lied she *was* exhausted. Which was amazing considering she'd only been up an hour. The only thing she'd done was eat breakfast, then scroll through a few personal emails and Facebook before Robert called. To be honest, she was surprised to hear from him. Last time she had spoken to him was by text, thanking him for a flower delivery almost two weeks ago.

The day she had spent with him had been fun. He was a good conversationalist, and had a habit of making her laugh. They both perversely enjoyed trying to get under the other's skin. It was nice to be able to tease and play with a man who was secure in taking a joke. While she had loved her birthday outing, plus the wonderful sex that followed—she once again was thinking they should put an end to their fling.

"Don't think about him today. R&R is the only thing on your agenda." Gathering water and snacks she hunkered down on the couch. She started flipping through channels, randomly stopping on a game and started eating her chocolate covered Crunch n' Munch. She zoned in and out for twenty minutes, sometimes watching TV and other times checking her phone, when her doorbell rang.

She shifted but made no attempt to get up. It rang again and she ignored that too. If it was a salesperson they could rot for all she cared. When the banging started she jumped up so quickly, she almost tripped on a pillow laying on the floor. She stalked to the door heated. She just wanted to rest on a Saturday for goodness sake! She jerked open the door without even looking.

"There better be an emergency—" She trailed off as she saw who was actually standing on her step. "Didn't I tell you now wasn't a good time? If you came to get some oh well because I'm on my period."

"Hello to you too. That's not why I came by. I was bored and wanted to chill."

"You a damn lie but that's okay, I'm going to hold you to it." She waved him in and shut the door. "Come on in. You on house arrest for at least two hours, since you just want to *chill*."

"Fine with me." Robert took off his boots and coat, before following her inside to the living room. He had been surprised to see her open the door in some loose fitting sweats and a looser fitting sweater. She still looked good but this was the least dressed up and unstylish he'd ever seen her to date. He'd taken her for a 24/7 fashion plate. "What game you watching?"

"Not this one," Mika said irritably, already turning to a movie she remembered passing. "I want to watch a romantic comedy." She was going to make him suffer, for once *again* coming to her house out the blue.

"Now who a damn lie," Robert said dryly.

He knew she was being contrary just to spite him. He was lucky she hadn't thrown something at his head. He was a man who'd grown up with two females. He understood that sometimes, their periods turned them into crazy people. She finally found the show she wanted before stretching out fully, plopping her footie covered feet in his lap. He got comfortable and then pulled out his phone.

"Why don't you understand how to take no for an answer?" Mika grumbled.

"Just part of my DNA I guess. Folks who do don't go far in life," Robert replied still distracted with his phone.

"No, you're just annoying. Your mother didn't beat your behind enough."

Looking up he grinned at her. "I got my fair share. But I wasn't trying to make my mother's life harder."

"Right now, I find that hard to believe. Put your phone down, I'm supposed to be torturing you with this stupid movie."

"I will in a minute. This app just got done downloading. Okay, which day of your period is this?"

"What?"

"Is this day one, day two? How long does your cycle usually last?" He asked his questions slowly, as if she might be having a hard time understanding him.

"Day two," Mika answered before she caught herself. "Why in the world are you asking me this?"

"So I can track it in this period app." He swung his phone briefly to her so she could see, then back around to enter the info. "Are you five days or seven?"

"None of your business. Why in the world are you tracking my period?" Mika was outdone. She didn't know whether to laugh or hit him.

"You don't take pills, so I'll go with the average which is seven days," he mumbled to himself.

A few seconds later he was done, placing his phone on the table. "What do you mean why? You're not on birth control, and we're sleeping together. Like I've told you before, I don't do kids. I might as well track you, it's another way to know your least fertile days. Condoms of course will still be used."

Her mouth gaping she stared at him. He said everything so nonchalantly and technically he had a point. "You are such a methodical stalker."

Suddenly she was tired. She rolled her eyes at him once and flopped back down. She had never met a man so comfortable talking about periods. Grown men often fled the room whenever a hint of a woman's bodily function was mentioned, as if the cycle didn't give life to their ass. If she wasn't having mild cramps she would have found his outlook refreshing.

Robert allowed the conversation to drop and they both watched the movie. It was sappy, but luckily funny as well. At some point he started massaging her feet, and that elicited a groan of pleasure so he kept at it. He knew some women were funny about a man touching their feet. He had never understood why. Even the worst woman's feet couldn't compare to a man's. Sure, he could admit sex had been on his mind when he'd called. However, he had no problem shifting gears and relaxing for the afternoon.

Not thirty minutes after he started she was fast asleep. He finished watching the last few minutes of the movie and of course the couple got together. Turning off the unrealistic movie for a sports channel, he settled back and watched the updates as she shifted onto her side curling up. He absentmindedly rubbed her lower back while she sighed and slept on.

When Mika re-opened her eyes blinking groggily, she saw an extra bottle of water and Robert's cell phone but not the man himself. She hated her period. The foggy mind and tiredness was the antithesis of her normal self. Her flow would be coming down in earnest before the night was over. Checking the time, it was almost four pm. She slowly sat up holding her stomach. Yep, the real deal was on the way.

"My bad, did I wake you when I got up?" Robert asked walking back into the room.

"No...yes. I don't know, and it doesn't matter." She stood up and handed him his phone. "You did good, I release you from your sentence. Now get out, so I can shed my uterine lining in peace." She started pushing him towards the front door.

"Okay, okay I'm gone. You sure you good?" He asked stepping into his boots as she handed him his coat.

"Yes Robert. Thank you for the concern and the foot massage, but I've handled this thing called a period all by myself for a long time."

His phone rang and after a quick check he answered. "Hey man, hold on a minute."

To Mika he said, "I'm leaving. Lock up and get some rest."

"Sure thing Dad. Drive safe and stop showing up at my house before I sick my neighborhood watch on you."

He only smirked as she shoved him out the door. He heard the lock click and started walking to his car, belatedly remembering Cam was on the phone.

"My bad man. What's up?"

"What's up with *you* is the question? Who house you leaving?"

"A friend."

"Hmm." Cam was trying to figure out if he was going crazy or not, but figured there was only one way to find out. "Funny, but your friend's voice sure sounded like Mika's." Cam waited for Robert to tell him he was wrong...and waited. "Fuck, Robert. What the hell?"

Robert transferred the call to his car as he pulled out the driveway, "Yeah, it was her, so what? We kicking it."

"Define 'kicking it'. How long has this been going on?" If Cam hadn't been so caught up in all the changes in his new life, he probably would have noticed sooner that Robert hadn't mentioned dating anyone in months.

"We really about to go through this?"

"Humor me," Cam said tightly.

"We hook-up, have sex from time to time just in case you need clarification. It's been going on for a while."

"Why didn't you say anything?"

"Because it wasn't that big of a deal, and it still isn't. It's an every once and a while thing. No strings on either side."

"A mutual agreement huh?" Cam's vague anger dissipated as he pondered this new development.

"Yes, an explicit mutual agreement. There was no room for confusion. Look you cool with this or...?"

"If ya'll on one accord, it's all good. I mean I'm surprised but we're all adults. Still don't know why you never mentioned it."

"Not really your business," Robert countered.

"Yeah whatever. I bet Andrea knows."

"I'm thinking she doesn't...otherwise you would have."

"I guess you right on that. Is this a secret or not?" Cam asked.

"I wouldn't say that. I just think neither of us were thinking about either of you, when we made our decision. Except in the beginning when we were trying to figure out if it was worth it or not. We could barely stand each other. Neither of us is looking for a relationship, particularly with the other. Just some fun when the mood hits."

"I won't touch the part about you two not liking each other but still sexing. I can mention this to my wife then?"

"If Mika hasn't told her...I wouldn't go telling a woman's business."

"Just great! The first secret I'm keeping from my wife is that her best friend is sleeping with mine."

Robert laughed over the connection. "Well, at least the first one is a good one."

Chapter Thirteen

Mika hated the annual New Year's Eve Gala that she had to parade herself to. That didn't stop her from liking the charity it helped. S.A.Y Detroit was a foundation of major programs to improve the lives of Detroit's neediest citizens. From cradle to career, and beyond. With its educational, medical, housing and career programs. A worthy cause her mother and father had started championing four years ago. Not long after her mother became a board member and attendance had become mandatory.

If nothing else she'd been taught the old-fashioned rule of never publicly embarrassing one's mother. So each year she came, even allowing her mother to pick out her dress—and the man whose arm she was supposed to dangle on. This year's date was Stanley MacKenzie. He was a president in the making for some company. She hadn't bothered to remember since meeting him casually last year at a different event.

Mika's mother was always setting her up. This is where being an only child really sucked. No other sibling for a meddling parent to turn their attention to. Her mother had that old-school mentality that "respectable" women needed to be married with kids. Even those with careers were expected to squeeze in a husband and a kid or two.

Mika wouldn't have minded the "setting up" part so much if all the men her mother picked weren't so *cookie cutter*, which meant boring and conceited. The men barely asked her anything about herself, and usually found her a little *too* colorful and modern for their wishes. They wanted

99

their woman to be mostly seen and not heard. Oh they believed a woman could be successful in this day and age, just not *too* successful. Can't outshine their man at the end of the day.

To bad for them, as she had no intention of dulling her shine for anyone. She thought any woman could get behind that type of thinking. Not so when it came to her cousins, who were currently looking at her as if she'd lost her mind. They were circled together off to the side talking. They all wore light-colored dresses as being extra bright would be considered gaudy. Forget that this was supposed to be a party. Her cousins Michaelle, Misha, and Milissa thought she was making much ado about nothing. Sometimes with all their names being so similar it was hard to have a conversation with them all at once. When they were kids if one of their parents messed up their name they would just say, "You know who I'm talking to!" To make it slightly easier she had started going by Mika and Milissa was often called Lissa. They all had names that started with "Mi" in memory of their grandmother Millicent. Who had died before any of her grandchildren were born.

"Honestly Mikala, what is your problem? Stanley is a good catch," Michaelle said sipping her wine, and looking as if she was about to hear a story she'd heard many times before.

"Agreed," Lissa added, her eyes scanning the room. "But I'm sure she'll tell us momentarily what defect he has."

"Get over it already. Give the man a test drive before you write him off completely," Misha her favorite cousin interjected, before discreetly eating the olive off the martini she had just demolished.

"Mother tried pushing him at me last spring, but I wiggled out of the few attempts he made to connect," Mika replied.

"Well maybe you should try him out tonight."

"Misha I doubt he'll think I'm wifey material if we sleep together on a first date."

The cousin in question just grinned. "I slept with my husband on our first date. You got to know how to put it on them little cousin. Besides, thought you weren't looking to be anyone's wife? So what do you care what he thinks?"

Lissa interrupted before the two got into one of their squabbles. "I'm still waiting to hear the defect. What's wrong with him to *your* mind?"

"You mean besides his blandness, and the fact he's a presumptuous prick? He thinks the night is going to end the way Misha is talking. Just because mother set this up he's been treating me like it's a sure thing."

"It's New Year's Eve, and you're at a party at a hotel. I think most of the men here are hoping their night will end with a bed partner." Michaelle waved away Mika's excuse. "The man has money, comes from good family and is almost at the top of his career. Plus, he's not yet forty. You should seriously consider him. You're running out of options in the Metro Detroit area with the way you keep tossing them aside."

"So I should just saddle myself to the first successful black man with a little money and status that looks my way? Even if they're boring and annoying?"

"Of course not," Misha spoke seriously. "We're looking for a man with a *lot* of money and status. Also don't forget one who is good in bed. We may as well get an extra perk for our trouble."

As the cousins shared a laugh at her expense, Mika shook her head. "I can't with any of you. I want more than a good fuck. I can get that anywhere. I want a man who keeps my interest, looks at me with passion and care. Not like I'm another *asset* he's acquired on his 'black and successful' checklist."

When they all just looked at her oddly, she'd had enough. "Forget it, I need a drink. And if Stanley asks you where I went, be kind for once and point him in the opposite direction."

Robert labeled attending these types of fancy parties under "work". Oh it wasn't mandated by the job in any way, wasn't even hinted at. However if you were smart you went where the money was. Sure, it was a tame versus the New Year's parties he had gone to a few years back. But what better time to talk rich people up, than when they were drunk and happy? He got to spend his time telling jokes and getting a few high-end clients and leads. While in this case helping a good cause and eating and drinking expensive food.

He'd been here a little over an hour, and it was now a quarter after eleven. Robert figured he might stay until twelve-thirty or so, depending on how the night was going. On average he preferred leaving early to beat the real drunks to the road. As he extracted himself out of a loose group conversation, he figured he'd head to the bar and get his last drink of the night. He was halfway to his destination when he stopped dead in his tracks. He saw a backside across the room that he recognized. He had palmed it, slapped it, caressed and squeezed it. Hell it had been the first view he'd ever had of her. But the rest of what he saw wasn't computing for his brain.

She was standing in a small group of women, who even from this distance he figured had to be related. Super straight hair in various shades of brown fell to the small of her back. Not a curl or kink in sight. He had always liked the highlights and lowlights that played in her hair. Her dress was silver and beaded in various patterns around her body. When she turned to address a member of the group, he was able to tell the dress had a split that came up to her knee on one side. Knowing Mika the front probably dipped enough to show a bit of her breasts. He had never seen her in anything so colorless, though he found no fault in the fit of the gown. It was a true shock that she was here tonight. He watched her turn abruptly from the conversation and walk away. Before he knew it his feet were moving to intercept her.

Mika didn't know why she had expected her cousins to have any sympathy for her. They mostly thought like her mother and aunt, feeling that she should find a good prospect, pick one and settle down already. Marching across the room with no clear destination in mind but to get away from them *and* avoid her date, she suddenly felt the tiny hairs on her arms stand up. Stopping mid-stride she did a graceful pivot on her heels and saw him bearing down on her.

Her jaw wanted to drop, whether from surprise or how good he looked, she didn't know. He was decked out in his expensive, cobalt blue Tribeca tuxedo with black lapels. His beautiful dark chocolate skin showing to advantage against the color. There was nothing like a black man in a suit or evening wear! But this was almost too much to handle. What was he doing here? When he got close enough, she asked around the knot in her throat.

"You taking this stalking thing too far Mr. Lorde." She chided. "What's your middle name, so I can file my PPO in the morning?"

Robert gave a slow grin. He'd been wrong, while the dress did in fact bare her shoulders, every tempting inch of her breasts were sadly covered.

"Not everything is about you princess. I came here to milk some rich men and women out of their money, and of course to help our citizens in need. What are *you* doing here? I barely recognized you." He ran his eyes from her head to her toes. The outfit *on her* was ultra conservative in his opinion. Even her jewelry was sedate.

Mika frowned a little. Why'd he'd have to look at her as if she was odd? She fit in and looked just as presentable as all the other women. Her mother had made sure of that.

"My mother is on the board, so I came to support. *And* so she can make sure I'm seen by all the rich men you want to take money from."

"Ahh, she's trying to pawn you off on some unsuspecting Daddy Warbucks."

"Something like that. The only requirement being he's rich. Being successful is optional. I'm pretty sure she'd take old family money," Mika said dryly.

"Smart woman, at the end of the day money is money. It's not so much how you get it, but what you do with it once you have it."

"I'm greatly disturbed that you have something in common with my mother."

Robert only chuckled, stepping closer. "Anyway, you look good." She looked beautiful, elegant, classy...almost untouchable. "The hair is unexpected but nice."

"Thank you. You're doing that tuxedo justice as well." If he looked any better in it, women might start fainting.

"This gentleman certainly is. It's an excellent cut on him."

Mika actually cringed, stiffening as the voice continued. "Mikala, won't you introduce us?"

She saw his brows rise in amusement at her given name. Suppressing a sigh, she slanted her body to allow her mother into the conversation. "This is my mother, Beverly Harrison. As I mentioned she's a board member of this wonderful organization. Mother, this is Robert Lorde. Andrea's husband best friend, and my new financial advisor."

Shaking Beverly's hand Robert said, "I no longer have to wonder where *Mikala*...gets her beauty from."

Beverly almost let a full smile come to her face before catching herself. "I thank you on behalf of us both for the compliment, and for attending our event tonight. The money raised will help a lot of people."

"Indeed it will," Mika's father said as he came upon the group, putting his arm around his wife.

Mika watched as the two men introduced themselves. Most men might find Reginald Harrison III a little intimidating. He stood 6'3" feet tall and had wide shoulders. His caramel face was often serious if he was focused on business. Right now it was relaxed and open. She was sure the drinks he'd had throughout the night helped. Plus, as her father neared retirement age he became less stern, while the opposite seemed to be true for her mother. Regardless she needed to figure out a way to move this little party along. Before she could do that, she was alerted to someone coming up behind her by the stiffening of Robert's shoulders.

She turned to see who it was, and went right into the arms of her stale date Stanley. "Oh!"

"I apologize for my neglect. A few people started talking in-depth business and it was hard for me to get away." Stanley said giving her waist a squeeze. Behind her Robert's eyes tracked the movement.

Mika had nothing to say as she wasn't particularly happy to see him. As the two younger men gave each other curious stares, her mother clearly gave her a look that said she should be introducing Stanley. Mika pretended not to see it and after a beat or two of extended silence, her mother did it for her. Mika let the conversation float over her head. She simply wanted to be home, celebrating the New Year in her bed away from *all* annoying people.

When Robert caught her eye she ignored the question in them, but also finally untangled herself from Stanley's arm. Her mind registered the conversation only when she heard her mother say, "Robert we'll have to have you, Cam, and Andrea over for dinner sometime."

Before Mika could protest *that* idea, a striking, tall woman appeared at Robert's side.

"There you are. I see you ran into another conversation as I was dying of thirst."

Mika's eyes snapped to Robert's before appraising the woman fully. She was a lovely shade of dark cocoa powder and was slim in all the places Mika was not. Which helped make the dazzling red dress she had on hang beautifully on her model-like frame.

Robert acknowledge the woman's presence but made no move to introduce her. In fact, he made his excuses to the others quickly and turned his date away. With a nod over his shoulder in her direction he said, "Mika."

"Robert," she replied, and watched him walk off with the woman, as her mother watched her.

As the clock crept closer to twelve Robert tried to focus on the conversations around him. He'd finally gotten the drinks for himself and Evonne, and they had made their way around the room to mingle some more. Five minutes to midnight he found his eyes on Mika and her date. They were standing in a cluster with the same women he'd noticed before.

When the countdown started he ignored the shouting crowd and the many flat-screens around the room. No, he wasn't paying attention to the D-Drop in the city. His eyes were focused solely across the room as he watched Mika enthusiastically join in. When midnight struck the cheers got louder, and people toasted and kissed all around the ball room. He watched she hopped up and down a little before Stanley caught her face for a kiss. Robert also watched as she didn't pull away. Empting his glass of champagne in one gulp, he turned away from the sight.

Chapter Fourteen

Robert must have lost his damn mind. He was sitting outside her house wondering where the hell she was. It was almost two am! He had driven way out to Troy to drop off Evonne, who had been silent and sulky since leaving the party shortly after midnight. That was fine with him. That pompous ass putting his lips on Mika was running in his head on repeat. He'd seen the dirty bastard palm her ass too.

He'd texted her several times already. Asking when she planned to head home, what plans she had for the rest of the night, and did she want company? No reply. He would bet a c-note that Stanley had gotten a room for the night. Right now she could be in that room taking off that dull-colored dress for him. Not that he should care, right? Which didn't explain why he was clenching his phone so hard?

Mika was about five minutes from home, and she'd never been so happy. She had been fighting off Stanley since the New Year rang in. He'd caught her off guard with that kiss. When she had finally pushed against his chest, he had just laughed still caught up in celebrating. About fifteen minutes later her mother had given a short speech, before encouraging folks to have fun until the event ended at three a.m. By that time she was on her water-only kick, and dodging Stanley's grabby hands also helped her quickly lose her buzz.

When she wasn't playing "duck a lip" or "slap a hand" she attempted not to wonder where Robert was in the crowd.

Had he been kissing his date as the clock struck? A woman he wouldn't even introduce her to. Mika wondered if he was afraid she might flip out over him having another bed partner? He needn't have been concerned. She had more class than that. A quarter after one she started saying her goodbyes, eventually Stanley had walked her out attempting another kiss.

"I'm sorry, but I told you I have a headache."
"Forgive me, I didn't mean to be thoughtless. I booked a room for tonight, didn't want to be drinking and driving. You're welcome to come up and lay down until your head feels better." He said all this while stroking a finger along her bare shoulders. *"And once you feel better, maybe we can continue the night together. Get to know each other."*
"Not tonight. I appreciate you being my date for the evening however. Maybe we can meet for lunch sometime. I have your card...I'll call you." Translation—hell no and don't call me, I'll call you.

As her garage door lifted she pondered what that said about his character. That he was "willing" to wait out her headache to get some? These were the men her mother thought would be perfect husbands? Folks who looked shiny on the outside but sucked on the inside. Luckily her headache had started to dissipate the moment she'd gotten in her car, proving it had been the people around her causing the issue.

Making it to the living room she kicked off her shoes and was throwing her coat over the end of the couch when the ringing of the doorbell made her jump.

"What the hell?" Picking up the clutch bag she'd tossed, she took out her phone in case she had to call for help. She stood there waiting, hoping it was just a drunk person at the wrong door. When the doorbell trilled again she went to the kitchen and grabbed her pepper spray out the junk drawer. She finally looked at her phone intending to enter 9-1-1, so all she had to do was press send. That's when she noticed the three texts from Robert, sprinkled in with well wishes from a variety of friends and coworkers. Quickly she read them and knew it would be him at the door.

She looked out the peephole anyway to check. It *was* him glaring at the door, her porch light showing he had no coat or gloves on. What was wrong with her that every time he showed up at her house angry, she found him deliciously sexy? Maybe because he reminded her of a sleek black panther, ready to pounce at any moment. All that restrained energy was enticing. Like the excitement you felt inching to the top of a rollercoaster.

"What do you want?" She called through the door.

"To talk to you in the house and not out here in the cold."

"I don't feel like talking," she said tiredly. "I'm going to bed. Go home Robert."

There was a long pause before he said slowly, "Open the door Mikala."

At the use of her full name she almost swung open the door and pepper-sprayed him. Instead she returned the tempting spray to the kitchen, leaving the phone on the counter too, before going to open the door.

"You have five minutes. It's late and I want some sleep."

"Okay." But once he was fully inside, he made sure the door was shut and locked.

She took a few steps back. "What do you want?"

"Where were you?" He said quietly looking around.

"Robert you know where I was—same place as you. I'm *really* not in the mood for this. What did you come here for? Don't you have other people to bother tonight?"

He ignored the reference to Evonne. "Why didn't you respond when I texted you?"

"For the same reason I haven't responded to the other thirty texts I got. I haven't checked my phone in hours," she snapped. "Also I'm not *obligated* to answer every time you text, call or whatever. I have this big other life that doesn't include you. Just as you obviously have friends...outside of me."

Up until that point Robert had been standing with his hands in his pockets, looking everywhere but at her. He finally caught and held her eyes. "Her name is Evonne and we haven't been together in well over a year. She's just a friend."

"Okay." She blinked, shifting. "Whatever. I'm still not clear why you're in *my* house right now or what you need from me this late."

"I need this."

Striking like the panther she'd compared him, to he closed the space between them pulling her roughly into his arms. She opened her mouth to protest and that was the last breath she took for a while. He ravished her mouth in a deep claiming kiss, there was no give and take, he just took and took more—overwhelming her senses. She stumbled back, constricted by the slim fit of her dress. Robert caught her only to spin her around, pushing her back until she met the wall.

He pinned her there pushing his leg between hers, until she had no choice but to widen her stance for balance. He had one large palm already squeezing a breast by the time she finally wrenched her lips free.

"Just...what...do you...think you're doing?" She asked between gasps for air.

"You asked me what I needed. This is it." He trailed his tongue down her neck to her shoulders before lightly biting the exposed skin right above her breast.

Mika jerked in surprise but before she could wrap her mind around that, he was running his hands down her body, shaping her as he lowered himself to his knees. Then he grabbed the split of her dress, ripping it up her hip with easy strength.

"My mother bought this dress!" She shouted asininely.

"I'll buy you another one." His voice was deep, serious and aroused as he ripped her panties clean off as well. The small scrap of material flying across the room. "This dress was too plain for you. Didn't do you justice."

"You've lost your damn mind...you—" She lost her voice as his tongue licked her clit, her head snapping back to thump against the wall. Within a minute of him twirling his tongue and strongly sucking on her nub, she felt her knees give out. Only grabbing at his shoulders kept her upright.

She fought to breathe her dress suddenly too tight, her nipples hyper aware of the material against them. The damn man used his tongue like a paintbrush, licking deep into her folds, spreading her wide for even more access. Dipping into her wetness, re-wetting his brush before doing it all over again. Her legs started to tremble, and no words were able to leave her throat. When she glanced down to watch this powerful, intense man pleasuring her, it sent her right over the edge. She came shivering, bucking and calling out his name. "Robert!"

His only response was to give her a long lick upward that had her convulsing again. When she started to slide down the wall he pushed her back up and *continued,* as if she wasn't already boneless. She grabbed a fist full of the hair she loved, trying to anchor herself against an overload of sensations. She let her head fall back again deciding to enjoy the ride. She lost sense of time and didn't know how long it was before she heard the crinkle of a condom wrapper. She struggled to bring her mind into focus as his mouth never stopped. The next thing she knew he was up and so was she—literally up against the wall, her legs reflexively wrapping around his hips.

He paused looking into her eyes, before leaning in for a much more measured kiss than the first. Not only taking but asking her to give. Give to him what he needed, what *she* needed and *craved* in this moment. So she gave, putting all the craving she had for him into *her* kiss. Making it known she wanted him and wanted him *now*.

Robert accepted lowering her down onto his shaft in one stroke. As she cried out, he shuddered at the feel of her closing around him. The need he'd delayed since entering her house sprang forth, his hips pounding upward as she clung to his neck for all she was worth. He was near-mindless—only knowing that he needed to be inside her—a part of her.

He sucked at her collarbone needing her skin in his mouth, but he wanted more. He'd love to have one of her succulent breasts in his mouth. Trying to make it happen, he took a hand from beneath her and started pulling at the top of her dress. Without saying a word Mika reached up and behind her unzipping the dress a few inches. Trying to wiggle the snug material down and off her arms. The extra movement made him groan, and he went back to holding her up. Fighting to make sure the pleasure didn't buckle his *own* knees.

When she freed herself from the dress and strapless bra, Robert suckled on her eagerly. Mika felt every pull in her belly, all the while he pumped strong and sure inside her. She didn't know how much more she could take, even as she used her feet against his ass to urge him on. She felt it—a climax rising in her. That pleasurable ache that coiled low in her belly. His strokes became harder and faster which seemed almost impossible at that point. When he sharply bit her nipple, she let go and shattered around him. Her cries still echoing around the silent house as he followed her over the edge.

Robert hadn't cum that hard in a long time. It drained him of his passion *and* his strength. He put one arm against the wall to help stay upright, which caused her to slide down even more on his softening but not yet gone erection. They both let out a groan, his knees half-buckling before he felt the sting of Mika's nails in his neck.

"I swear, if you drop me I *will* pepper-spray you."

He felt the tension of the night fade, as her comment assured him they were back on familiar ground. He used the last of his strength to lift her up and off, lowering her to the floor. There she stood dress ripped near to her waist, top sagging down nearly as far. He felt his dick twitch with renewed interest and sought to distract himself. He stepped back, a man fully-dressed in formal attire not counting his pants being around his ankles.

"Do you think I can see your actual bedroom this time?" Robert asked breaking the silence.

Mika didn't answer him. Instead she freed herself from the dress and bra, letting both items fall where she was. Stepping around him she went in the kitchen and grabbed her phone and a bottle of water, drinking half of it before coming back out. He was just leaving her guest bathroom and met her in the hall that led to the stairs.

"I'm not sorry about the dress," were the first words out of his mouth.

"The replacement better be expensive, and I betta like it."

"I'll make sure it's a better fit for you, some color, some flair. That dress tried to tone you down."

Mika thought that was one of the sweetest compliments he could give her, but didn't tell him that. "Whatever, as long as it's expensive. I want you to *feel* the sting in your wallet. You also owe me a pair of panties." She pushed past him and started up the stairs.

"You never answered my question. Am I spending the night?"

"Yeah fine, whatever." She turned pointing a finger at him. "To *sleep*. I told you I was tired and I have an early morning tomorrow. Neither of which you cared about when you barged over here."

Robert thought about trying to look contrite, but he wasn't. He started following her up until she pushed him back.

"No, you can come up *after* you go clean up that heap of clothes you demolished."

"You not letting it go about that dress, huh?"

Mika grinned at him evilly before walking up the stairs.

Chapter Fifteen

Mika eyes popped open when the alarm went off at 9:45 the next morning. She *soooo* wanted to go back to bed! She was physically and emotionally drained. Mostly due to the man who had his heavy arm around her waist. They'd slept naked, their body heat enough to keep them warm during the cold winter night. Now in the morning light she didn't want to examine last night, not yet. Right now she was still a little angry and a lot confused. Figuring it out would have to wait, she had more important things to do this Sunday morning.

She removed his arm and got out of bed, which woke him up. When she was sure he was cognizant she said, "Get up. We need to leave in around thirty minutes."

"We?" Robert asked sleepily.

"Yes, we. I have someplace I need to be and you're dropping me off." She gave him a look that dared him to object.

"O-kay, how you getting back home?"

"Not your business. Chop, chop."

He watched her naked ass walk into the bathroom then heard the click of a lock. He was not looking forward to a morning of her attitude. But a smart man knew when he was on thin ice and learned how to tiptoe. Damn his cousin Edward for being right.

* * *

Mika refused his offer to make her a quick breakfast, *and* the coffee he'd brewed. So imagine how pissed he was when she made him stop at a McDonalds once they reached downtown. She proceeded to order four large coffees and twenty-five various breakfast combos. Rubbing salt in the wound when she told him if he wanted something for himself, he should order it. *Then* she made him pay for it all!

She also refused to tell him where they were going, parceling out directions as they went. By the time they parked in the back lot of a medium size building, his irritation had skyrocketed along with his curiosity. She piled most of the bags of food in his arms, taking the coffee herself as they walked through the back door.

"Where are we exactly?"

"You'll see."

"Mika..." he said exasperated.

She just ignored him.

He shook off his annoyance and continued through the complex. Taking a look around as he went. He saw various rooms in different sizes. A few were clearly offices. The rest he saw had some books and what looked like school supplies in them. In another room, he glimpsed what seemed to be a pantry of sorts. Clothes, purses, and jackets were organized on racks. There was a shelf of bins that held deodorant, toothpaste, tampons, etc. He wrinkled his brow, trying to figure out exactly where they were. When they walked into a gym-like area with a handful of lunch tables set up, it became clearer.

"Hey girls! Happy New Year! I got breakfast. Hurry and come get it. Then take your seat. We're going to have a special presentation this morning."

Mika put what she held down on a table, taking off her coat. Then telling Robert to place what he had a little further down on the table, as the 15 girls were already rushing him.

As he was mobbed, the ladies made their way over to her. Andrea was giving her a look that said, *What the fuck?*

While the other two were eye molesting Robert and grinning at her.

"Happy New Year to *you*. *I'd* be happy if I started the year out with him!" Kimberly said fanning herself as Mika handed her a coffee and a bag.

"Where do you find these fine men? I need to hang out with you more. Damn girl!" Julia complained.

"He's just a friend," Mika mumbled around a bite of her own McMuffin.

Kimberly choked on a sip of coffee as she tried not to burst out laughing. "You a damn lie," she said in a near whisper. "You didn't come here with your 'friend', who is still dressed in a full tux from last night."

Julia was shaking her head as well. "Whether friend or *special friend*, what's his name?"

For the first time Andrea spoke up. "His name is Robert...he's Cam best friend."

"You two make me sick. Greedy, monopolizing all the men," Kimberly said pouting.

"Why is he here?" Andrea asked briskly.

"You guys just have a seat and you'll see," Mika said looking at her phone to see it was indeed eleven a.m. on the dot.

Mika stepped forward addressing the girls, clapping her hands to grab their attention. "Okay ladies, you can finish eating as we have our first lesson of the New Year. As you can see we have a guest today, who also happens to be a male. This is Robert Lorde, and he'll be demonstrating a few ways a man should treat a lady. He even got dressed up to make it more realistic. I would have done the same, but there was an unfortunate accident with the dress I planned to wear."

Mika saw his eyes pop in surprise, then narrow at her dig. She had to bite her lip to keep from grinning. "Ladies let's give him a warm welcome to The Growth & Hope Center."

Robert walked forward slowly, a loose smile on his face. Oh he was going to get her back somehow. He didn't know when, just that he would. So far she'd used his money and outed their connection to Andrea, who still looked like she had entered the Twilight Zone. Now she was making him perform so to speak, in front of a room full of teenage girls. Half of which couldn't stop grinning and giving him sly looks, while the other half looked at him warily. While he walked over, Mika grabbed a chair and sat it at the table.

"Let's start with how a gentleman should get your chair for you when you're on a date."

Robert obliged her. Pulling out the chair and waiting until she lowered herself onto it. Before also helping to push the chair in closer to the table.

"Why you gotta have help to sit? Thought ya'll always telling us to be independent women and s-tuff." Tamara caught herself before she cursed.

Before any of the women could speak up, Robert did. "Because it's not about you being capable, which you are. It's about a man showing you basic respect. When a man is helpful in big or small ways, it shows that he cares for you. If a guy can't show you basic respect in everyday aspects of your life, that means he's thoughtless."

All the girls were attentive, as he'd used his "no-bullshit" look along with an edge to his voice.

"Mr. Lorde is absolutely right."

Alysia a shyer girl, raised her hand. When Mika smiled and pointed to her she said, "Ms. Harrison, what if the guy honestly doesn't know he's supposed to get the chair? What do we do then?"

Mika rose replacing the chair, then shooed Robert off to the side. "Well you should stand by your chair, then look pointedly at your date. You can give a slight head nod to the chair if he still doesn't get it." She demonstrated and Robert played along, looking oblivious as she stood there until she nodded her head. Hustling over to get the chair to the girl's giggles.

"It's okay to stand your ground. It's important to set the tone for how you want to be treated early in a relationship. Don't you agree Robert?"

There was a slight pause before he said, "Yes."

She stood up and went over by the door, motioning him to join her.

"Also, whenever walking on the street with a man, you should be on the right. The farthest away from the street."

Mika and Robert linked arms and strolled across the room.

"Again it's a sign of care and respect." Mika explained. "With you on the inside, you're more protected. From mud splashes or a car jumping the curb."

"Do we have to link arms like that all the time?" A girl shouted out, her voice clearly appalled at the thought.

Mika laughed. "No, not unless you want to. You can just be walking side by side or holding hands. Doesn't matter as long as you're on the inside."

They ran through a few more examples. A man holding the door open. How a man should shorten his stride a bit, so a woman doesn't have to work extra hard to keep up. They demonstrated that if a man saw a woman was cold, he should loan her his jacket, assuming he had one. When Robert undid his tux and took it off, she heard a few giggles from the girls and Kimberly mutter loudly, "This is too much *and* not enough!"

For the final demonstration, she had him sit down at the table where the other ladies were at before she entered the room. "Lastly young ladies, if you enter a room and there is no seating left and a male is seated, he should *happily* give up his seat once he's noticed you need one...right Robert?"

He reluctantly said yes, reminding himself this was all for impressionable young girls. He was aware she was pointing out his flaws. Truthfully a lot of these tips were similar to what he had drilled into Brihanna. Teaching her to demand respect from everyone, in particularly men. He got the message, and after last night could admit he deserved it.

"Okay ladies, that's it for our Male Manners class. Let's give Mr. Lorde a round of applause for helping us out today."

The girls did so, as Robert gave a small bow.

"Now," Mika continued. "Take fifteen. Clean up breakfast, then we can start on your vision boards."

Tamara was all smiles now, having warmed up to Robert. "Can he stay and help us with our boards?" There were murmurs of agreement around the room.

Andrea stepped forward and shook her head. "Sorry girls. Robert can't stay for that. Some things are girls only. Vision boards are deeply personal, and we want everyone to feel comfortable. So you can really put what you feel on the boards."

Amidst the groans of disappointment, the adults met at the head table, where Mika finally introduced him to everyone.

"Thank you so much. This was a great lesson for the girls to learn, especially from a guy," Julia declared. "I could tell they took you more seriously than they take us."

"Yep, they consider us 'old'. As if we couldn't possibly know anything about male and female interactions," Kimberly put in. The other ladies agreed sharing a laugh.

"Not a problem ladies. I'm glad I could help. I'd actually like to come back and talk to them about financial responsibility and investing, if you think that would be okay."

Julia's eyes lit up as she was an accountant. "Absolutely! Let's cover basic budgeting first, and then you can move to investing!"

"We'll look at our schedule for the year and make sure to get you in. Should be able to give you plenty of notice," Kimberly said making notes in her planner.

"No worries." Robert said easily. "I'll make time whenever you have a spot for me. These two know how to reach me." He indicated Andrea and Mika.

"I sure do. Let me walk you out," Andrea offered.

Mika followed the two as they headed toward the back door, the girls waving goodbye to Robert.

Robert slung his arm about Andrea's shoulders and made conversation. "How you doing A? How was your first New Year with our boy?"

"A?" Mika questioned from behind them. "You actually let him give you a nickname? Is there anything you *won't* do for Cam? You *hate* nicknames."

Andrea threw a dirty look over her shoulder. "Robert didn't give me much choice, and it grew on me." She turned back to the man by her side. "We had a good time. Kept it in house with our own little party. We had hats and everything. Along with a *lot* of champagne."

"I bet he got you another piece of jewelry, didn't he?"

Andrea let out a laugh. "Yes! You really should talk to him about that. He won't listen to me."

"I've tried. Damn boy will end up broke." Robert exaggerated a big sigh. "Guess I'll have to do my job better and keep making him money."

Andrea gave him a quick squeeze as they neared the door, then stepped back bringing the group to a stop. "You do that. I was surprised to see you...but you did a great job with the girls."

"I was only supposed to be dropping Mika off." He gave Mika a half-amused, half-annoyed look. "You'll get her home?"

123

"Of course." Andrea's eyes danced between the two, before she shook her head a bit. "See you later. Mika don't forget you told the girls fifteen minutes."

Mika had her arms crossed, staring seriously at Robert. "I know what I said, I won't be long."

Biting her tongue not to snap back, Andrea turned and walked away.

Alone, Robert grew more serious as well. "I get it. Your lessons."

"Good. It seemed to me you needed a refresher."

"Point received and taken. But to be fair I never said I was a gentleman."

"That's obvious. I'm telling you to *do better*," Mika said firmly.

He slowly closed the distance between them and pulled her in for a hug, folded arms and all. Stepping back he gave her a quick kiss. "I hear you princess."

She finally cracked a smile and gave him a shove towards the door. "Get out of here before I figure out some other way to torture you. And put on your damn coat. I don't play 'nurse and patient'."

He was still laughing as she shut the door in his face.

Chapter Sixteen

On the drive home Andrea kept up casual conversation about the girls, her night with Cam, and her new jewelry acquisition. Mika played along with her, even though both women could feel the tension in the car. Andrea's mind was racing a mile a minute. What was going on with her friend and Robert? She wasn't afraid to ask, just wanted to wait until they got off the highway.

Mika kept from rolling her eyes by looking out the window whenever she could. She knew Andrea was dying to find out about Robert. She also knew her friend was probably waiting for the right moment or hoping Mika would volunteer the information. She hadn't been thinking clearly when the scheme to teach Robert a lesson popped into her mind. Figuring if he could come to her home marking his perceived territory like a caveman; then she could display him in front of whoever *she* wanted. She just hadn't thought about the conversation she would have to have with her best friend after the fact.

Andrea parked in Mika's driveway, but left it running for the heat. She turned as Mika unbuckled her seatbelt.

"Thanks for the ride. Sorry to make you come all the way out here."

"The ride...is not the problem."

"Is there a problem?" Mika testily asked.

"Should there be a problem?" Andrea responded in kind.

"No, so I guess there isn't."

There was silence. Andrea softened her tone and asked even though it felt awkward. "So...how is he...*you know*?"

"Fantastic of course. Why do you think I'm dealing with him?"

"Really? He seems so serious, a little bit reserved sometimes."

"He can be." Mika smiled a little. "I'm going to call him 'focused' and that can be a very good thing when it comes to the bedroom."

After another unnatural pause Andrea turned forward in her seat.

Mika was still tired, having used up her limited energy on the girls. She just wanted to get this over with, followed by a long nap.

But Andrea beat her to it snapping around in her seat to ask, "So, what exactly is going on with you two? Are you dating? A couple? What? How long have you been seeing each other?"

"It's been going on a while."

"What's a while Mika?"

"A few months give or take."

"What! Why in the world didn't you mention this?"

Mika shrugged defensively. "I don't know. I mean I didn't think it was a big deal at first. I figured we'd get sick of each other, and it would fizzle out."

"Apparently it didn't, and you still never said a word." Andrea knew Mika's excuse was crappy. The woman *always* mentioned whoever she was dating, no matter what.

"When did it become *mandatory* that I tell you everything? We're hooking up, it's not a big deal."

"Oh, so you bringing 'hook-ups' around the girls now?" Andrea said in disbelief. "What was that show this morning about since we on it?"

"That was me reminding myself of something important *and* teaching the girls some life lessons at the same time."

When Andrea rolled her eyes and shook her head, Mika felt her temper spike. "Just what is your problem with this anyway? Why do you care if we're sleeping together?"

"Because he's Cam's best friend! This could get real messy."

"He's his best friend not his daddy. We're both adults. Any blowback is not your problem."

"Oh bullshit Mika! You know that's not true. If you hurt him, it will affect us all."

"If I hurt him? What do you mean by that?"

"I mean I know he's not your type and I know you don't keep a guy around for long. I just don't understand why you didn't pick someone else to play with instead of my husband's closest friend!"

"Wait just a damn minute! You acting like Robert is some soft, callow schoolboy and I'm some pedo teacher who has lured him into a sexual trap." Mika was livid. "He is a grown-ass man, older than us both in case you missed it. His reputation with women is not so shiny either. We both agreed to be booty-calls to the other. *No one* was taken advantage of, least of all him. I'm *your* best friend. But you don't seem to be worried that I might get hurt!"

Andrea threw up her arms. "Because you don't take relationships seriously! From what I saw this morning you got that man's nose wide open! The Robert I know would *never* have let you puppeteer him like you did this morning. You claiming it's just hooking up, but maybe it's more to him. I mean you spent New Year's Eve together!"

At the mention of that fiasco Mika had enough! "You know what? I'm done! You are out of line, it's not your business and you need to mind your own!"

Mika threw open the car door and got out.

"Well *that* I believe, since you hid it from me for months! Sounds like a guilty conscious to me!" Andrea yelled right back. She instantly knew she had gone too far when Mika's features hardened. Her friend slammed the door before stomping into the house without another word.

* * *

Mika had slept late into the evening on Sunday, and when she woke spent the next few hours with her headphones on immersing herself in work. Anything to keep her mind occupied. When she got tired of that she took a rare sleeping pill and slept until Monday morning. They had the day off since the holiday had fallen on a weekend. She spent it with her phone turned off, eating junk food and binge-watching action movies. Late Monday she finally returned her mother's call and completely ignored the texts and calls from Andrea.

Being back in the office on Tuesday was an actual relief, though all anyone could talk about was the holiday. *She* was trying to forget about hers. At around noon a flower delivery arrived. A single huge, purple Hydrangea. By three the receptionist was escorting another delivery person to her office.

This time with a fairly large box, expertly wrapped. She opened the card first.

Trust...I felt it
R.L.

She knew it must be the dress. How in the world had he been able to find something between Sunday and Monday? Shaking her head she lifted the lid and gasped. Inside was a ruby red gown. The top portion wasn't exactly like her last one, this one hanging *just* off the shoulders, creating a C shape on her chest. The cut was lower and would expose the top swell of her breasts but still be tasteful.

What caught her eye were the jewels that lined the silver collar, alternating rubies and diamonds—*real ones*—across the whole arch. Lifting the dress out the box she stood up to see the rest of it. Like the previous dress it had a split to the knee. At the waist there was a two-inch silver band that would make the shape of her hips and behind stand out. The band was littered with crystals and more rubies thrown into the mix. There was *nothing* muted about this dress. As she was about to repack it she noticed there was a small bag in the box. Shaking the contents out to reveal a pair of ruby red panties! They were so skimpy Mika assumed they must be for decoration only. She hurried to fold the dress back into the box and texted him.

Mika: You can't send something like this to my job!
Robert: Yet I did
Mika: Half the office is breaking their neck to see what I got
Robert: Did you like it?
She loved it, but refused to tell him that.
Mika: It looks expensive...so it will do
Robert: I'll call you tonight

She didn't respond. At this point, she didn't know whether she was looking forward to talking to him or not. But she loved her dress!

* * *

Cam set Andrea up in a nice bubble bath with a glass of wine. He figured that would buy him at least thirty minutes of peace and he could make his call. She had come home on Sunday from her Center meeting in a bad mood, waving him off when he asked what was wrong. Then Monday rolled around and she was clearly still upset, as he watched her mumbled to herself when she thought no one was listening. By dinnertime he demanded to know what was wrong.

Andrea had narrowed her eyes at him and then pointed an accusing finger. "I bet you knew, didn't you?"

"Clue me in."

Her eyes narrowed even more, if that was possible. "Two words, Mika...Robert."

At that point about ten different scenarios had flashed through his mind. All with three basic themes; lie, evade, or tell the truth. Apparently, he took too long to decide.

"Why didn't you tell me? How long have you known?"

"Easy baby." Cam threw up his hands. "Only about two weeks or so."

He cut her off as she went to speak again. "I didn't tell you because they don't need our permission to...do whatever the hell they're doing. If Mika had wanted you to know, she would have told you."

Her mouth had opened then snapped closed, her shoulders sagging in defeat. "I'm sorry. I'm not mad at you. I just don't know why she wouldn't trust me...share what was going on in her life."

"Don't take it so personally."

"What other way am I supposed to take it?"

His wife had been sad and a little mopey ever since. Now it was Tuesday night as Cam closed the door to the spare bedroom downstairs and made a call. When Robert picked up he said, "It's finally happened."

"What did?"

"There's been a girl fight."

"Really? Andrea and Mika", Robert asked.

"Yeah, who else would I care about? My wife's been either angry or sad since Sunday."

"Hmm." Robert rubbed his temple.

"What did you do?" Cam asked.

"Me? I didn't do jack."

"I know it's over you. She called me out on knowing about you two. Plus, Mika won't take her calls or return her texts."

"Damn, she's *that* mad?" Robert would never understand women.

"Apparently." Cam would never understand women either. He just knew his wife was unhappy and he didn't like it. "You need to fix it. I don't like seeing sadness in my wife's pretty eyes."

"Hell, I'm not a hundred percent sure *I'm* out the doghouse!"

"So you did do something," Cam said sternly. "Find a way to make this right."

"I'm on it. I'm supposed to call Mika tonight anyway."

"Good luck."

Robert hung up and shook his head. Women made everything more complicated. Getting up he poured himself a drink before calling the complication.

"Hey," he said clearing his throat as she answered.

"Hey yourself."

Silence from two people who normally never ran out of things to say.

Mika finally said, "We should talk about what happened after the party."

"We def need to. I believe in addressing things head on." He took a big drink. "I'll apologize if you want me to. But deep down I'm not sure I'd change anything."

"Oddly, I don't think I would either. We needed a catalyst to have this talk." Mika agreed.

He felt most of the tension leave his shoulders, he stopped pacing and took a seat.

"What set you off?" Mika asked. "I mean we both had dates. It shouldn't have been that big of a deal."

Robert hadn't known this would be *so* uncomfortable. But he hated bullshit, even from himself. After a long silence he answered, "I didn't like him touching you."

"What? Him having his arm around me?"

"No. I saw him kiss you at midnight."

"Oh!" Mika paused, letting his words sink in. "I didn't even know you were close by."

"When I saw that, I'll admit I lost it. Gave in to irrational jealousy. That's how I ended up at your house."

A small part of her was thrilled Robert had felt the need to claim her. "Nothing happened with him except that kiss. He tried to get me to go to his room. I firmly declined and went home. Where I was confronted by an angry man, who had *no right* to question me like he was my father."

"Oh I think we know I'm not your daddy. About these rights—"

"You don't have any," she cut him off crossly. "Remember? No obligations, free to see and do whatever we want with others."

Damn women for remembering everything. "Look, you know we've progressed beyond that."

"Do I? Just because you got jealous for a hot second doesn't mean anything. That could be normal possessive man shit."

"Be real. You were jealous too, until I set you straight about Evonne."

Mika sucked her teeth before saying, "Whatever."

"Look let's modify the original agreement. Take off that last part."

"So we take out the other people, but keep the no obligation part...really?"

"You right." Robert was in uncharted waters, but he refused to sink completely. "I suppose we can upgrade our situation to 'casual, exclusive dating'."

"Oh, that's real benevolent of you," she said sarcastically.

"Okay, how would *you* like to phrase our current situation?" When he was met by silence, he growled, "Mika don't ignore me."

"I'm not! I don't know either...this is..."

"Unexpected," he finished for her. Softening his voice he continued. "Which is why I think we should take measured steps for now. No pressure, just casual exclusive dating." He paused to let that sink in. Hell for himself as well. "You game?"

Mika bit her lip to stop a smile from spreading, even though he couldn't see it. "Bet."

"Also, you need to drop this beef with Andrea."

The smile left her face as quickly as it had come. "You *had* to go and ruin it."

Chapter Seventeen

As the first Saturday of January rolled around, Mika was cautiously hopeful. Since their talk Tuesday night, she and Robert had communicated every day in some fashion. Often by text or even an email. Sometimes a short call. Nothing excessive but way more than before. They were currently on their way to lunch at a spot downtown he liked. She could add "day dates" to the positive direction they were moving in. It had been a good week, except for him pestering her to talk to Andrea. Talking to her best friend about this new development would be great, shame she was still pissed off.

When they reached the restaurant she thought it was odd he didn't wait to be seated but continued straight through the place. Until they rounded a corner and she saw Andrea and Cam sitting in a booth. Cam stood up while Robert pushed her stunned body down.

"You two, talk," Robert said pointing at them both.

"And where are you going?" Andrea asked Cam.

"Away from here. Work this out." Cam handed her the car keys. "I'll text you where we're at later, and you can drive over...together."

"Let's head out." Robert said checking the time.

Mika spoke up for the first time. "I'm adding liar to your title," she said peevishly.

"Nope. I said I was taking you to lunch and I've brought you to a restaurant at lunchtime. I didn't lie," Robert stated before turning and walking away.

Cam tried to suppress a smile at the interplay between the two. Leaning towards Andrea for a kiss he was rebuffed as she gave him her cheek. He took what was offered then moved on, giving Mika's shoulder a quick squeeze. "Be nice, Trouble."

"You should have told your *wife* to be nice, then maybe we'd be speaking."

On that note, Cam hurried from the table.

"And *you* should have picked up the phone or responded to my texts instead of being childish," Andrea flung back.

"Now I'm childish as well as being a cold-hearted bitch?"

"I never called you that!" Andrea huffed leaning forward indignant at the accusation.

"You might as well have. You insinuated that I'm some heartless chick just out for myself, randomly playing with men's emotions. That I was somehow taking advantage of Robert."

"Are you ladies ready to order?"

"No!" both women replied at the same time. Watching the waiter drop off the two waters before backing away.

They sat staring at each other until finally Andrea broke the silence. "I said I was sorry about the way I handled things. You could have responded."

Mika picked at a napkin. "You hurt my feelings, I was too mad to talk."

"Well, you hurt mine too!"

"What? How are *you* the injured party?" Mika asked genuinely confused.

"Because you kept this from me! You've never kept a man you were fooling with a secret. Hell you've overshared, sometimes even when I asked you not to. I mean I don't understand why you suddenly cut me out of a big part of your life...for months!"

"I just...I didn't think it would still be an issue down the road. I expected this fling with him to burn out quick." Mika pushed her hair back. "I personally didn't want you to get your hopes up that our little group would turn into a happy foursome."

"You tell me about your flings all the time. What was different?"

"Yeah but neither of us wanted things to be super awkward if things went really bad. I didn't even like him at first, we just have this crazy attraction."

"Are you ready to place an order? Maybe some appetizers at least?" While the waiter's tone was pleasant enough, it was clear he expected them to actually order some food. They both took a quick look at the menu and relayed their choices.

As the waiter left Andrea hesitantly asked, "You said you didn't like him at first. Does that mean you do now?"

"Yeah, I guess I do." Color flooded her face.

"Wow, is that the unflappable Mika Harrison blushing over a guy?" Andrea laughed in surprise. "I think you *like* *him*, like him."

Mika held up a hand. "Hold your horses. I'm not admitting to that at this stage."

"Whatever. It's starting to make a little more sense. Start at the beginning. Tell me *everything*."

Mika had missed being able to talk about this "relationship" with someone. "Okay. But you have to promise not to get upset."

"Why would..." Andrea cut herself off. "Okay, I promise."

"The beginning starts in Vegas. We slept together then."

"You what!"

"You said you wouldn't get upset," Mika reminded her.

"I'm not upset but I don't understand why you didn't tell me," Andrea whined out the question.

"You were on your honeymoon! Plus, I could barely believe I'd slept with a man I hadn't even known for 24 hours."

"But you can send me Karma Sutra poses? You thought crossing the line would be mentioning you'd slept with the best man?" Andrea quipped.

"What can I say, I'm not selfish. I didn't want to make it about myself. The poses were for you and Cam. I know you used a few of my ideas though." Mika naughtily smirked.

"Maybe." Now Andrea was blushing. "I can't believe it goes back that far. Is this serious?"

"I don't know. It's hard to explain. We had no contact once we got back. Didn't see each other again until you dragged me to that game at his house."

Thoughtfully Andrea nodded. "So I wasn't imagining the tension in that room when we found ya'll?"

"No, then we slept together again a little after that."

"And now?" Andrea prodded.

"We've recently upgraded to actually dating. Lord, help us both."

"That's a good thing right?"

"I'm cautiously optimistic." Mika gave a small smile. "You pointed out before that I've never been in any *true* relationships."

"I didn't mean—"

Mika cut her off. "You were right. Thing is, I don't think he has either at least not in a long time. I don't think either of us knows what the hell we're doing."

Andrea smiled at her. "Feeling lost and confused sounds like the start of a relationship to me." She reached out and grabbed Mika's hand. "Don't overthink it. I'm sure you told me that a time or two with Cam."

Mika squeezed her hand back. "Try about a *dozen* times."

The women shared a laugh, and over their meal all was forgiven. Mika brought her up to speed filling in the blanks of the last few months. Doing her normal oversharing which had Andrea alternating between covering her ears, and leaning forward for more. Andrea paid the bill as another way to show she was sorry.

Fanning herself, Andrea took a long sip of water. "I'll say this...if nothing else you two seem to have a *healthy* sex life."

"That's one statement I can't dispute."

Just then Andrea's cell beeped. "It's Cam. He gave me the address. Are you ready to go?"

"Yeah, I'm ready to go scold Robert for his deception."

* * *

Robert and Cam had grabbed a quick bite to eat at a drive-thru after leaving the women, before heading to the gym. It had been a while since they'd last went a round or two. Robert had been all for it when Cam had included it in their plan. Both men were looking forward to the hour they had rented the ring out for.

While getting dressed they talked about the odds of the women working it out. Both were stubborn when they wanted to be. At the end of the day they figured they had done their part, and now it was up to the ladies.

Robert was in blue gloves, while Cam wore red. The two men spent a good five minutes warming up with a few jabs and stretches. There was no one there to referee, but the ring had a clock you could program for up to twelve three-minute rounds. They could also program the standard one-minute break in between. Of course they were not professionals and could use the time in the ring however they wanted. Robert was looking forward to releasing a little aggression. The week had been stressful and dramafied—two things he detested.

"You ready to bring it?" Cam asked circling him, warming up his footwork.

"Everyday baby! Less talk, more action," Robert responded.

Cam gave him what he wanted and moved in for a quick strike that Robert barely avoided. Robert refocused and before he knew it three rounds had passed. Trash talk was abundant during the brief breaks, in between guzzling water. They both seemed to be a little more out of shape than usual.

Women...a distraction on so many levels.

Is what Robert was thinking when Cam slipped under his guard and caught his jaw with a solid right hook that rocked him back and had him holding his face.

"Damn! That felt personal."

"It was," Cam grinned.

"What the hell for?" Robert was moving again, striking out but only landing a glancing blow to his opponent's shoulder.

Cam shook his head and ducked under a powerful fist coming his way then got Robert with another good shot to the ribs, before saying, "You know you're *in* it now."

"If I didn't know it before." Robert caught Cam with a good jab to the jaw. "I know it now."

"Don't hurt her on purpose. Whatever ya'll doing, whatever ya'll got...even if it ends, do it right." They both swung and missed. "Mika is a good woman."

"I know, and I won't." Robert said tightly. Breathing hard from all the talking and moving. "Although, I'm getting really tired of folks *teaching* me lessons."

"Ahh, Mika getting you together already?" Cam chuckled, forgetting to protect against the hard hook that landed in his stomach.

Luckily the timer rang, and both men had apparently had enough. They backed away and focused on breathing. Even ignoring the signal that their one-minute break was up. Eventually Robert took the first steps forward. He hated being schooled. At the same time he was glad to know Mika had someone solid and loyal in her corner.

He held out his gloves. "We good?"

Cam pounded gloves with him nodding. "Always."

Andrea drove them to a rather large gym complex located downtown.

"What are we doing here" Mika let out a light chuckle. "Did they plan to make us fight it out or something?"

"With those two who knows?" Andrea joked. "But I think it's more likely they're here working out."

Mika nodded, taking in the various stations as they walked through the place. She saw it had some work-out equipment, a corner where folks were doing kickboxing and a room that looked like a small class was practicing Judo. Interesting.

"How are we supposed to find—" Mika trailed off as they entered the second section of the building. "Holy crap, are they boxing?"

"Oh yeah, Cam mentioned they do that from time to time." Walking closer to the ring Andrea frowned. Whatever she expected it wasn't this full on fight she was seeing.

A delighted laugh bubbled out of Mika as she hurried to reach the ring, right as Cam landed a punch to Robert's chin. "Good one Cam!"

Her shout startled both men who turned towards her as the bell rang, ending the round.

"You cheering *him* on?" Robert scowled down at Mika.

"Not exactly. However, I admit I got a little tingle of satisfaction when his fist connected."

"What exactly are you two doing?" Andrea asked appalled.

"What? I told you we box." Cam said confused, as he shuffled his feet.

"But I didn't think you guys were literally beating the crap out of each other. He has a split lip and you have a bruise starting on your shoulder!"

Both men looked at each other and shrugged. They didn't see a problem.

Mika waved away Andrea's concern. "Oh let them fight. How much time do you guys have left?"

Robert looked at the wall clock. "We could probably get in another two rounds, if we weren't standing here talking."

"Camden..." Andrea sounded worried.

"It's all good. In fact you come stand in my corner and cheer your man on." He gave her his most charming smile, which had her laughing in defeat.

"I always got your back love, but I don't want to hear any complaining tonight when you're sore and aching." Andrea admonished.

The two men went back to fighting. With the women encouraging them from the sidelines, wincing when extra-hard hits landed. If both men were being honest, they probably fought a little rougher with their women watching.

When the round ended Andrea entered the ring fussing over Cam, giving him water. Mika handed Robert a towel while hanging over the ropes.

"You want to know something?" She said so quietly he had to lean forward.

"What?"

"I am finding you *extremely* sexy right now."

"Finally something I want to hear today." Robert mumbled watching her eyes roam his body, instantly feeling a twitch of life down below.

"Too bad we're not somewhere I can show you my real...appreciation."

"I can solve that real quick." Robert wasted no time turning around and addressing Cam. "What do you say we call it a day?"

"Exactly what I was thinking." Then Cam said to the ladies, "Give us fifteen minutes to shower and we'll be right out."

They parted ways the men making quick work of getting cleaned up. When they came out they didn't see the girls and thought maybe they'd gone to the front. They headed that way, stopping in a doorway when they saw Andrea. Mika was inside sparring with an instructor. Robert watched her spin, block and advance in awe, until he finally found his voice and stepped forward.

"What martial arts is this?" He whispered to Andrea.

"Hey you two. Oh this it's Aikido. Mika is a 4th degree Kyu. I told her she should work her way up a couple more degrees, as she has a talent for it. I stopped at the first stage," Andrea responded nonchalantly.

"You can do that?" Cam asked, pointing in disbelief.

"Not really. I know a very few basic moves. I ended up being better with a gun, so I focused on that and Mika continued with this. This Judo instructor was nice enough to help us pass the time with a little friendly bout."

Robert was fascinated as he watched the concentration on her face and the graceful and quick moves she employed. He knew without a doubt that Mika Harrison would never let a man do anything she didn't want—not when she could lay him flat in probably fifty ways. Something he would keep in mind as they moved forward. One thing was for sure, she was a constant surprise to him.

Chapter Eighteen

A week after she had made up with Andrea, Mika went to visit her parents. They lived in Canton as well, though thankfully far enough away from her. It had been her childhood home from the time she was five. Her father had become one of the first African-American Directors at Ford. Promptly moving his family from Detroit to the suburbs. Her mother had decided the location wanting to be closer to her only sister Jacqueline, who lived there with her family. By the time Mika turned eleven her father was a VP, increasing his workload and wallet even more.

Her mother Beverly had been a schoolteacher and continued to work in the Detroit school system for another thirteen years after the move, retiring when Mika graduated from high school. Mika had found that ironic, as right when she finally didn't need her mother she suddenly had more time for her daughter. Mika had grown up in a big home, going to private schools, where she and her cousins helped make up the 2% of non-white faces that walked the halls. School had been messy only in the sense that she didn't conform like so many other people of color.

By the time she was ten, she refused to let her mother hot-comb or perm her hair. Letting her natural curl pattern do what it wanted. As soon as she got to junior high where her school didn't require uniforms she played with colors, textures and styles while most people around her were wearing Abercrombie and Fitch. She'd been the girl with the colored scarf on her head, sometimes in African wrap methods that caused her teachers and classmates to stare. But other than a few cultural bumps, she had enjoyed school. She'd had plenty of friends of all races, was fairly popular, and got involved in anything that remotely caught her interest.

Mika had done it all! Theater, track, debate team, art classes, afterschool computer classes, French, and Spanish. Even spending a year in glee club. Anything to keep her busy and not at home where it seemed like her mother was always pushing her to be different. A 4.0 was good, but why not aim for the 4.2 and 4.5 they were starting to give students? Her look, activities and manners had been constant things the two disagreed on. Her mother had always been proper, but moving from upper middle class to upper class had put her into overdrive.

Beverly for a number of years had tutored her students after school. Was on *any* committee that was trying to improve the district. When she retired, she'd gotten on a variety of boards throughout the Metro Detroit area. Mika could admit Beverly set an excellent example of giving back to one's community and trying to raise it up. While at the end of the day her mother never forgot her true roots, her motivation had been twofold. She wanted to be the perfect wife to compliment her husband's new status. Mika gave her props for staying socially and professionally active, instead of becoming a trophy wife.

Mika knew she was a daddy's girl. Being his only child meant she had been spoiled from the start. Add in his guilt for working long hours at work and when at home, meant he usually gave her whatever she asked for. He had sided with her often which was how she gained the freedom to be *different*.

He seemed honestly thrilled by her spirit, while her mother was only concerned with how her actions might cause her to stick out. Reginald had never been embarrassed, and would proudly introduce her to all as his beautiful and talented daughter. If Mika was being honest, as much as she played down her rich and privileged life it had helped her in many ways. One of her dad's counterparts having known her for years, actually secured her fellowship at a top company before she graduated college. The place she'd met Andrea and gained a friend for life. Money definitely smoothed a path in life.

Funny enough her mother loved Andrea, and felt she was the perfect modern lady. Fairly low-key, and more demure than Mika ever hoped to be. Her mother probably thought she would be a calming influence on her daughter. To a degree she had been. Mika had added some adventure to Andrea's life, and Andrea had added some stability and sisterhood to hers. Andrea didn't look at her and see dollar signs or connections, nor did she see a weird black girl that didn't *quite* fit in with the normal black-girl narrative. Andrea had just seen a person who she wanted to be friends with, had accepted her for who she was. More accurately the young adult she had been, who was growing into her own.

Mika shook off the thoughts as she knocked on her parents' door. The reminder of her beautiful friendship had her getting a little misty. Ugh, what was wrong with her lately? Seemed every time she turned around she was getting emotional in some fashion. Is this what nearing thirty did to people? God, she hoped not.

After she sat with her dad catching up and watching an hour of sports, she went to have tea and dessert with her mother in the kitchen. So they could have what her mother always said was *girl time* talk.

"I saw Stanley return to the ballroom after you left...I had hoped you two would hit it off."

"He wanted to hit it alright." Mika mumbled.

"Excuse me?"

"He was nice enough mother, just not my type."

Beverly barely suppressed rolling her eyes. "Funny, in all these years I've yet to determine just what *your type* is dear. Feel free to enlighten me."

"Drop it. Let's not do this today." Mika took a big bite of her macaroon.

"Okay fine." Beverly placated. "There was another matter I wanted to talk to you about anyway. I want to have that dinner I talked about, with Andrea and her husband. Camden isn't it? Preferably this month."

"She's probably too busy for dinner. They're still newlyweds, you know still adjusting."

"Nonsense. It's been a good five months. They should definitely be making their rounds together as a married couple. I had hoped to see them at the event."

"They had their own plans for the New Year," Mika defended.

"Obviously. I'd like to have them over for dinner. Will you be taking care of it or should I give her a call?" Beverly raised her eyebrow, letting her daughter know she was serious.

"Fine, I'll take care of it. Though I can't promise they'll have time in their schedule before the month is out."

Beverly waved away that minor detail. "I'm sure you'll work it out, so it suits us all. Also, don't forget to invite that friend of theirs...what was his name, Robbie?"

"Robert," Mika snapped. She knew her mother was an expert at remembering names. A necessary skill for an executive's wife, and the queen of chairing committees.

"Yes, that's it. I thought he looked familiar, now I know it was from the wedding video. Make sure he comes too. I like to keep my word."

"I'm sure he didn't expect an actual invite."

"Well he has one anyway. I know you don't know him that well." Beverly paused to see if Mika would tell her differently. "Since that's the case, I'd be more than happy to ask him directly. I'm sure I can get his information off the donor list from the event."

"No, I'll ask but I'm sure he has better things to do." Mika cringed at the thought of her mother having unfettered access to Robert on the phone.

Beverly smiled and nodded. "Good, it will be nice to have a small intimate dinner. I look forward to it."

* * *

That was how two weeks later in the last week of January, Mika found herself sitting outside her parents' house in her car with Robert. Listening to him sigh for the third time in the seven minutes they'd been here.

"Tell me again, why are we waiting outside?"

"Because trust me, you don't want to go in there before the others arrive. My parents can be a bit much."

"They seemed nice enough at the gala."

"Oh that was in public. This is on their own turf."

Robert laughed. "You make it sound like war."

"With my mother, it is," she muttered.

"This is stupid. You can stay out here if you want. I'm going inside." Saying so he got out the car.

"Damnit." Mika took a deep breath and got out as well. Luckily, before he could take more than a few steps Cam and Andrea pulled up, and the group went in together.

Her parents greeted them all in the foyer. Her mother giving Andrea a hug before turning to Cam.

"It's very nice to meet you. I was looking forward to meeting the young man who stole our Andrea's heart!"

149

"The pleasure is all mine. We appreciate the invitation. I hope you don't mind we brought a little hostess gift for you." Cam handed her a square blue and gray box.

The top lifted up easily, and Beverly saw it was a set of thank-you cards from the Smythson brand. Her eyes lit up and she beamed with appreciation.

"How nice! But *you're* the ones who should be getting gifts." Beverly turned to Andrea. "Which of course I have a wedding gift for you before you leave. I was so surprised to hear you'd eloped. Doing something *that* impulsive is more Mika's speed."

"It's what we felt was right, and I wouldn't change a thing," Andrea said looking up at Cam, who gave her a squeeze.

"She was kind enough to put me out of my misery Mrs. Harrison."

"It was a lovely ceremony." Beverly smiled genuinely pleased by the young couple. "Andrea, your husband is both charming and handsome. If only Mika could find the same."

"Honey..." Reginald spoke up before mother and daughter could start an argument. "Let's go in for dinner, the kids didn't come here just to chitchat in the hall."

Mika and Andrea helped set out food on the well dress table. While her dad blessed the meal, Mika sat with a pinched expression. Her mother per usual, had gone overboard, setting out name cards, which placed each couple across from each other, her mother and father at either end of the table. Mika had a suspicion mother had purposely put Robert closest to herself. Mika got out her phone and texted Andrea that she hadn't told her parents she was dating Robert. Unfortunately, she made the mistake of holding her phone above the table.

"Really Mikala, please put your phone away while we eat."

Cam was outright grinning at her reprimand, like an annoying sibling. She started to protest but just wanted to get through dinner.

"Sorry, Mother."

"Yes very rude. People are too attached to their phones nowadays," Robert said nonchalantly, giving her a bland look then turning back to his food.

She kicked him under the table, but he didn't even flinch. She saw even Andrea was snickering behind her napkin at this point.

"Agreed Robert! It's so refreshing to hear someone from your generation think that way." Beverly paid him the compliment, and he gave her a big smile in return.

Mika thought about stabbing all four of them with a fork.

The rest of the dinner went well, and she took Cam off her revenge list since his easy charm had carried the conversation a good portion of the night. Her mother asked a hundred and fifty questions. By the end Mika was impressed by how Robert evaded or shifted the conversation whenever her mother got bold or extra personal with him.

When the meal was over the ladies cleared the table, even though both of the younger men offered. Her mother waved them off before her dad took them to the entertainment room to continue talking. When it was just the women in the kitchen her mother let the other shoe drop. Beverly started by congratulating Andrea again for finding such a *nice, educated, kind, handsome man* of means to marry. Her mother had been impressed by Cam's taste in jewelry *and* his budget for it.

Then she segued into how she was giving up hope for Mikala to find the same. How *she* seemed to turn all the eligible bachelors away without giving them a chance. That she hoped Andrea's luck would rub off on her daughter before she had to import a husband for her. Andrea listened politely and nodded in all the right places, trying to say as little as possible. While Mika gritted her teeth and remained silent, until her mother said this.

"That Robert seems nice. I like that he and Camden are close. Men of high caliber often associate with others like themselves," Beverly said to the young women. "He seems to be single, as well." Beverly lobbed that statement directly at Mika, giving her a look.

"He's okay, but he's not the getting-serious type. That's something he definitely doesn't have in common with Cam." Mika didn't want her mother entertaining the thought that a wedding was in the near future.

"Hmm, if you say so. Such a shame if true."

Andrea had stepped in and reminded her mother about her wedding gift, then off they all went to retrieve it. When Mika pointed out it was getting late they gathered up the men and said their goodbyes. As far as Mika was concerned it was an escape.

Reginald and Beverly waved the kids goodbye as they left the house.

"What do you think?" Beverly asked.

"Cam seems like a good man. They make a nice couple," he responded, putting his arm around his wife's waist and leading her back through the house.

"Not them. I'm talking about our daughter and that young man Robert. I think something is there."

Reginald leaned down to kiss her forehead. "As usual you're right. I think they're together."

"I don't know, both are hard to read. Mika is always so defensive around me, and he didn't give away much either. That one is *smooth*, almost *too* smooth." Beverly narrowed her eyes.

"The man is fine, seemed confident to me. Bold and not a pushover. The kind of man I'd prefer for our daughter."

"Hmm, maybe. Why are you so sure they're together?"

"They drove together then sat out at the curb, refusing to come in before the others showed up. That was my first clue. Guess they don't want us to know."

Reginald's wife might not have been able to read Robert, but man-to-man he could. The way he'd looked at his daughter throughout the night had instantly made him want to toss the man out the house. That was all *he* needed to know that something was going on.

"They did? I don't understand why she would keep it secret!"

"Beverly because *you* don't know how to stay out of her business. Promise me you'll mind your own and leave those young people to their relationship."

"I don't meddle. I just want what's best for her!"

"Promise me, you'll leave it be woman," Reginald insisted giving her "the look" he rarely used on either of his girls. *He* was usually a big pushover where they were concerned.

Beverly sighed and finally nodded her head. "Okay, I promise. I just hope it works out. He's the only man *I've* ever seen that she's shown some real interest in. I saw how she looked at him at the gala."

"You just have to wait and see how it goes. If it's meant to be, it will."

Chapter Nineteen

Valentine's Day fell on a Thursday this year, so she and Robert made a simple night of it. He brought over dinner and they had a relaxing night in. As a gift, she bought them Red Wing tickets for this upcoming Saturday. He'd been pleasantly surprised, as it had been years since he'd watched a game in person. It would be *her* first time going. She had never been able to bribe anyone else to go with her.

The weekend came quickly and saw them entering the new downtown arena with the rest of the crowd. They took a shuttle over after parking, as it was still too cold to walk. When it was time for the game they took their seats about mid-way up and settled in. As sports fans they were both decked out in red and white Red Wings apparel. Mika was looking forward to the game to come.

However, as the game entered its last twenty-minute quarter Mika was sure of two things. One she was drunk, and two watching hockey in person was boring. She could watch it at home no problem, but here she wasn't as hype as she'd thought she would be. That brought her back around to why she was drunk. Eighty percent of the crowd in the arena was buzzed or drunk too. The other portion was just naturally loud and rambunctious.

They had eaten dinner at Made In Detroit inside the arena, and had two or three drinks. Robert also got them drinks during both breaks as well. Honestly she had used them to warm up. Not one to take chances she had brought a red oversized throw inside, refusing to freeze her tail off.

Her voice was all screamed out, and she was tired of the frequent and unneeded fights on the ice.

Between the cold and drinks she was starting to doze off. That was until she felt Robert's hand rubbing up and down her thigh. She would take all the help she could get warming up. But when his hand dipped between her legs that jolted her awake! She looked around at Robert, but he was staring straight ahead, as if his fingers weren't dancing up and down the seam of her jeans.

She looked to either side and even glanced behind her. No one was paying them any attention. The novelty of them being a black couple in the stands had worn off during the first few minutes of the game. He pressed down hard rubbing in circles until she gasped, before he started over again. Mika went with it. She let the heat of arousal spread through her. The next time she shivered it *wasn't* from the cold.

Robert felt Mika's head fall to his shoulder as he continued his rhythm. After long minutes he could hear her breathing change, getting choppy. When he heard her low groan he turned his head to swallow her soft cries of release. He had never been so glad for a blanket, definitely needing cover for this erection in his pants. Robert was a little lightheaded to be honest. He hadn't attempted public sexual acts since he was a teenager. Something about her always made him act out of character. On second thought the fact that he was drunk might have had a hand in it too.

Mika broke the kiss as she got her breathing under control. Apparently something had happened in the game since everyone was yelling. She looked at the scoreboard and saw that there was just a minute left.

"You are bad."

"You liked it." Robert smirked.

"I'm going to pay you back for that."

"I look forward to it."

She packed up the throw, squeezing it in the small bag the arena allowed people to carry. "I'm going to hit the bathroom before the major rush."

"I don't need to see the end," he said. "Looks like we're going to win."

They got up and made their way out, a few other people were doing the same. They both took a bathroom break then started heading out with the rest of the crowd. She didn't know if it was the jostling crowd or what but she felt like everything was tilting. As they got closer to an exit there was one thing she *was* sure of.

The person behind her was grabbing her ass on purpose. The first time she chalked it up to the movement of the crowd, but the second time they didn't even try being subtle, just grabbing a handful. She made her hand into a fist and swung it back into the person's crotch. At the same time she brought her heel back and dug it into the person's toes. As he dropped hollering in pain, she grabbed Robert's arm and picked up the pace.

"What just happened back there?" Robert questioned.

"Nothing, had to deal with a grabby asshole."

"You want me to go back and beat his ass?" He offered calmly, dead serious.

"No, I said I dealt with it."

"Okay. It's cause you got on those tight, delicious jeans," he leered at her.

"It's because men are perverts."

"Yeah, that too." Robert agreed, pulling her aside when they reached the sidewalk. "Gotta be honest I don't think I should be driving. You up for it?"

Mika scrunched up her face giving the matter real thought. "I want to say yes because I want to get you to a bed, but honestly no."

"It's cool, I got another plan."

157

* * *

Cam had been coming back from the bathroom when he noticed his phone lighting up on the table. He was surprised to see a text from Robert, since it was after eleven.

Robert: Need fav bro, your house in 15

Now he was headed down the stairs to get the door after reading the latest text.

Robert: Pulling up now

He was reaching his hand out to open the door when someone pressed the doorbell, the sound ringing throughout the house. Annoyed, as he had been trying not to wake Andrea he snatched the door open, finding Robert standing outside with Mika.

"I'm sorry! I didn't know I wasn't supposed to ring the bell. How was I to know you had already texted Cam!"

"What the hell you two?" Cam hissed. "Lower your voice and get inside."

The couple entered and as Cam relocked the door they heard footsteps on the stairs.

"Cam baby, who's at the door?" Andrea asked, sleep tingeing her voice.

"Shit," he mumbled. Louder to Andrea he said, "It's Robert and Mika."

Andrea rubbed her eyes and came to stand next to her husband. "Are you guys okay? What happened?"

"We're okay. So sorry to wake you," Mika apologized.

Robert picked up their story. "We had more to drink than we should at the game, and neither of us felt we could drive home."

"We were hoping we could crash here," Mika said giving them her best winning smile. "Please?"

"We'll be out of your hair first thing in the morning," Robert tacked on.

Cam glanced at his wife for her input.

She yawned and waved her hand dismissively, "Of course you can stay. I'm glad you didn't drive. Do you want some coffee or anything?" Andrea offered.

"No, maybe just some water. We don't want to be any trouble, we're umm anxious to get to bed."

"Yeah I bet," Andrea snorted out a laugh. "Cam show them the spare bedroom down here."

"He knows where it's at." At the look his wife gave him Cam added, "But I'll show our *guests* anyway." Boy how life changed when you got a wife. Now he had to have "manners". In the past he would have waved Robert off to the room and went directly back to bed.

"How was the game?" He asked, opening the door to the room. He actually used the room as a library to store books, so at least two of the walls had shelves. However, there was a full-sized daybed against the window. There were some side tables and a small, simple desk in the opposite corner as well.

"It was good, colder than I remember. We won, so there's that," Robert replied.

"Cool, you parked in a lot right?" Cam asked. "I can take you to pick up your car in the morning."

"Yeah, I did. Thanks for letting us crash on such short notice," Robert thanked him. Mika was already looking at the books on the wall.

Andrea walked in and handed the waters off to Robert before setting down the towels she carried on a table. "There you go in case you need to freshen up. Also there's some packets of aspirin on top too, just in case. We have leftovers from dinner so feel free if you get hungry."

159

"Thank you sweetie, you think of everything." Mika gave her a quick hug. "We're all set, again sorry to wake you guys up. You should go on to bed. We're about to crash."

"Okay, goodnight." Andrea took Cam's hand as they left the room.

"Are you hungry?" Mika asked Robert as the door shut. He had his back to her taking off his coat and shoes.

"I'm good." He pulled off his jersey but left his undershirt on, it was a little cool in the room. Cam probably had the vent half-shut, since he didn't use this room often.

"Well, I am."

"Gone and get you something then." While he hadn't been tired when they left the game, now he was.

"I plan to." Coming up behind him she ran her hands up his chest, pressing her bare breasts into his back. "You gave me that appetizer at the game, but I want a full meal."

Robert got an instant shot of adrenaline and decided he wasn't that sleepy after all. Turning he saw her standing there butt naked. "Damn, you got undressed quick."

Mika laughed. "*Told* you I'm hungry."

He spun her toward the daybed. "Well I don't want it said that I don't know how to feed my woman." He tumbled them back onto the bed, and like a match striking into a flame they were all over each other.

A sudden intense need blazed in them both. They kissed, rolled, pulled and squeezed. The rest of Robert's clothes disappeared as Mika desire to see and feel his skin consumed her. She bit along his body, even scratching with her nails until he had to grab her wrists as he kissed down her body. He answered her need by loving her so well with his tongue and fingers that within five minutes, she was begging him to take her. She was delirious with need.

"Oh god, I need you inside me right now!" She flipped over and got up on all fours.

She didn't know how long it took, just that it felt like forever before he was pulling her hips back and pushing inside her in one firm stroke. They yelled out together at the feel of the connection, heat radiating along their skin. The cold of the room long forgotten. He pounded into her quick and steady, her hips matching him stroke for stroke. Her nails grasping and digging into the bedspread, the bed frame knocking lightly against the wall. Their breaths struggling for purchase in their lungs. And just like a fire starved of oxygen, it was over as quickly as it had blazed to life.

They both fell forward, Robert slumped over her. Murmuring in her ear he asked, "You full?"

"Yes lawd," Mika mumbled, a vague smile on her lips. "Sleepy."

And quick as a blink she was out.

Chapter Twenty

Mika woke up slowly, her eyes stickier than normal and her brain foggier. She was under the covers and she had no clue how that had happened. When she sat up the cold air hitting her naked skin did a lot to wake her. It also motivated her to get up and get dressed! She silently thanked Andrea as she grabbed a packet of aspirin, swallowing it down with the untouched water from last night.

She took her time finishing off the bottle as she was probably dehydrated. Mika vaguely wondered where Robert was, since everything but his coat was gone. As more of last night came back into focus, heat climbed into her cheeks. She loved when he took her from behind. The wildness of it, the depths he could hit! A wide smile overtook her face before slowly slipping off.

She had no memory of them using a condom. Most times he gave her the honor of donning him in latex, and when he didn't she watched. All she remembered was one moment his head was in-between her legs, and the next he was inside of her. Had they not used a condom? Oh god, he had been as drunk as she was! She rushed over to the trashcan in the corner. It was empty, not even a random tissue was in it!

"Fuck!" She said out loud, just as the door opened.

"You're actually up?" Robert teased flashing her a smile. "You okay?" He asked after seeing her expression.

"Did...did we forget to use a condom last night?"

"No, we're good. What made you ask that?"

"Are you sure? I don't remember you putting it on, or taking it off."

"You didn't *see* me putting it on and you wouldn't remember the taking-off part either. You fell dead asleep as soon as we finished. I almost did too." He walked forward perplexed by the entire conversation. "What is this about? I said we're good."

"Prove it to me. Where is it?"

"What the fuck is this inquisition?" Robert could feel his temper rising. Was she saying he was lying? "I don't have to prove anything. Why in the hell would I lie?"

"I don't know! Maybe because you don't want to admit that you were too drunk to remember just like I was, or admit you made a mistake." Hands on her hips, Mika started to pace.

"I never, *ever* forget a condom. I've told you that. And if I ever do I wouldn't lie about it. I'm a grown-ass man. I'd take responsibility for my actions."

"I know! But you were drunk. You might have—"

"Might have what? What does me being drunk last night have to do with me telling the truth this morning?" He couldn't believe they were arguing about this. "What would be my motivation in possibly getting you pregnant? I don't want your kid."

Well *damn*, that snapped her head back at his tone of disgust.

"Good, because I don't want you as my child's father either! Show me the condom if you not lying."

Robert turned and walked out the room, Mika hot on his trail as he went into the kitchen.

"Just show me," she continued, still trying to get visual proof.

"I'm not showing you shit. You got a lot of damn nerve. What do you think my plan was? To get the BAP pregnant as a come-up or something?" Both of their voices were raised.

"BAP," Mika muttered, as it took her a moment to realize he was calling her a "Black American Princess"—a kind of insult against black females who grew up rich and privileged. "Oh, fuck you! Maybe you did. I know you only really care about making money. You wouldn't be the first man trying to trap me for my family connections!"

"I don't give a shit about your money or your family connections!" Robert's voice was hard as stone. "I'm pissed you think I wouldn't protect us *both*. That I'd use you, and then lie about it all!"

Just then Cam and Andrea came down the stairs. They had heard the yelling from their bedroom.

"What's going on down here?" Cam demanded.

Mika was actually shaking, so she jammed her hands into her jean pockets. "Nothing."

"Didn't *sound* like nothing." Andrea put a hand on Mika's shoulder. "Are you okay?"

"Yes...no." She shrugged jerkily. "I don't know."

"But *I* do. *I* told you everything was fine," Robert snapped.

"That's what *you* say, not what I *know!*" Mika shouted back.

"This is bullshit and you know it." He was livid, moving forward and pointing his finger at her. "I would *never* do what you're accusing me of!"

Andrea stepped in front of Mika. "Let's all take a moment." She looked between the two before telling Cam, "Cam, why don't you and Robert go get us some breakfast from up the street. I'm sure this will be easier to figure out once we all get some food."

"Yeah, that sounds like a good idea," Cam said before either party could comment. Lips pressed thin he went over to Robert placing a hand on his shoulder. "Come on bro, go up to the Coney with me."

Robert didn't budge, just looking at Mika half-hidden behind Andrea. Finally he turned away. "Fine, I need to get out of here anyway."

Once in the hall Cam grabbed his keys and coat. Tossing an extra Robert's way, before they went out the door.

At the sound of the door closing, the air went out of both women. Andrea steered Mika to a seat. "Girl, what is this all about? You and that man looked like you wanted to tear each other apart—and *not* in the way you looked last night."

"I don't think he used a condom," Mika said, sitting with her head in her hands.

"What? Why wouldn't he? What did he say?"

"We were both drunk. I know I wasn't checking for one."

Remembering what Robert had been shouting Andrea asked, "But he said he used one right?"

"Yeah, but I think he's lying. He wouldn't prove it to me."

"Prove it? How...I mean...what did he say exactly?" Andrea was trying to make sense of everything.

"Since it wasn't in the room's trash, I asked him to show me. He said he didn't have to prove anything, that I should accept his word."

"Is there a reason you *wouldn't*?"

"I just can't remember him actually putting one on." Mika said sounding desperate.

"Okay, okay. Why don't we check and then you'll know. Did you check the bathroom?"

In her manic state she hadn't thought to go searching all the trash cans in the house. She got up and ran to the guest bathroom. Pressing the lid of the small trash can in the corner and there it was. Very visible *and* very used, sitting right on top. Her body sagged with relief, *overwhelming* relief. Dread was close on the heels of that feeling, at the things she and Robert had said to each other. She stumbled out the bathroom past Andrea who had been behind her.

"Well?"

"It was there." Her voice hoarse as she fought back tears. "Can you please take me home?"

"I can, but what about—"

"Please," Mika pleaded, her head and heart pounding.

Andrea bit her lip, she didn't think it was a good idea to run away while the man was out. Especially since he had been telling the truth. She hadn't separated them so Mika could duck out, but so the two could cool down.

"I'll get my stuff, but *I am* going to write Cam a note though."

"Thank you!" Mika sighed with relief, before getting up to retrieve her things from the spare bedroom. She couldn't deal with Robert right now. She needed some space and time to think.

As Robert entered Cam's house he was calmer. Cam had convinced him to just show her the condom in the trash and be done with the argument. They were just having a miscommunication, which if he put his ego aside he could easily clear up. They just needed to get back to her house and talk it out. While he was still pissed that she would think he had failed her, failed *them*—he tried to understand it was her knee-jerk reaction talking. His hopes of saving the morning in a civil manner was dashed when the women were no longer in the kitchen.

"Where'd they go?"

Cam shrugged. "Maybe Andrea jumped in the shower. Check your room for Mika."

Robert set the bags and coffee down and did what Cam suggested. He didn't find her nor any of her personal items. The room had been cleared, while his temper returned full force.

"She's gone." Robert announced coming back in the kitchen.

"I know, I just saw the message Andrea left. She said Mika asked to go home."

167

"Fuck, what the hell is her problem?"

"Calm down, maybe this is a good thing. Apparently she hasn't cooled off yet. Give her a little space."

"Oh, no doubt. I'll give her space alright." Robert's tone was hard and biting. "Do you have time to take me to my car, or do you want me to get a Lyft or something?"

Cam's shoulders sagged, he knew that tone. Robert wasn't open to being reasonable right now. "No no, I can do it," Cam quickly said. No way did he want to inflict Robert's current mood on some unsuspecting driver.

* * *

Mika wanted to curl up in a ball, but found herself pacing her bedroom instead. She knew leaving was only going to rile Robert up further, which had not been her intention. She just needed some space, some time to check her out-of-control emotions. Robert was a man and couldn't understand the fear a woman might have over an unplanned pregnancy. Financially there were no worries, having family support wouldn't be in question either. Though her mother would swear she did it on purpose just to buck her expectations.

It was the emotional part that terrified her.

Being responsible for one little human's world, their every need. Having the sole responsibility of shaping them into a productive adult, and not an asshole to society. Not to mention even in this day and age, people assumed *all* women wanted kids. Well, she wasn't sure if she did. Frankly, babies terrified her! She didn't really want to be around kids until they were about three. Her cousin Michaelle had a two year old son, who Mika had just started interacting with.

If she had to be a parent she didn't want to be a single one. For all that she complained about her family she loved them. She was lucky to have grown up with both parents who loved *her*. Even having extended family who annoyed her was a blessing. The few times she'd thought about kids, it had been having one in a *family* unit. Unfortunately, all the men she had "dated" would not be husband material, much less fit for fatherhood. They were barely fit to be *temporary boyfriends*. The thought of being connected to any of them for 18 years-to-life, sent dread to the pit of her stomach.

But Robert and a baby? She couldn't put the two together in her head, especially with her as the mother. They'd both only talked about their upbringing in little slices of conversation. She knew he loved his family, but would he ever *want* a wife or children? She'd gotten the impression he wasn't interested in either. She had no doubt he would *and* could monetarily provide for his child. That was only one aspect of being a parent. The day-to-day would end up all on her.

Not that she would expect a marriage just because a child came into the picture. That was weird and outdated thinking. No child needed to be raised in a home with two people pretending to care about each other, just so the "optics" would look right to society. She liked Robert and she honestly believed he liked her. In fact she liked him more than she had liked anyone in years. He was an intense man, he moved with purpose, figuratively and literally. She liked that about him. In other men it came off differently, as if it was all surface level. With Robert she had no doubt he'd earned every ounce of confidence he flaunted. How many times had he adamantly said he didn't want kids? His paranoia of babies rivaled her own. Which is another reason she should have known he wouldn't lie to her.

But it had been mere weeks since they decided to actually date. She could see them potentially having a real relationship, and that *alone* was scary. She didn't need an unplanned pregnancy on top of it all. Besides at the first sign of a potential mistake, she'd lashed out at him. He could be thoughtful, sweet and fun, all without being a pushover or boring. He didn't try to impress but to please her in ways that actually mattered. Other men failed to realize that since she grew up with money, she wasn't interested so much in the flash of it all.

She would apologize to him later today when they both had time to settle down. She'd try to explain her whacked-out thought process. She sat down on the bed just when her phone pinged.

Robert: So you just left?
Mika: I'm sorry I just needed some space, time to think
Mika: I'm so sorry. I know you were telling the truth. I saw the condom in the bathroom
Robert: You shouldn't have needed to see it, to believe me
Robert: You can have all the space you need from now on
Mika: What does that mean?
Robert: It means we don't need anything else to do with each other
Mika: That's not the kind of space I wanted, just a couple of hours to put things in perspective
Robert: I don't want to deal with a woman who has such a low opinion of me
Robert: We can work on transferring your accounts before the week is out
Mika: What the fuck Robert?

But that was it, she didn't get another text from him. The final straw to making her Sunday a complete failure.

* * *

Monday dawned overcast and gray with snow clouds and it mirrored her mood. Nevertheless, she took a late lunch and made her way over to Robert's office. She wasn't going to blow up his phone like some teenager. She figured she'd try to talk to him face to face. A single yellow Chrysanthemum had been delivered to her office today. What the hell did that mean? Well, she was about to find out. Peeking through the glass into his office she saw he was alone and not on the phone, so she did a quick rap on the door before stepping inside.

"Hey, can we talk?"

As Robert turned towards her his mouth tightened. "Shut the door."

She did. He stayed seated and she stayed standing.

"Now you want to talk? Thought you needed to run away and have your space," Robert said scathingly.

"Don't do that. Don't be a hard-ass about this," Mika implored, reminding herself to hold onto her own temper.

"You want to talk? Then do it quickly. I have nothing to say, and this is not the place to have this discussion."

"Okay first I want to make it clear that *I* did not ask for, nor do I authorize my accounts to be moved. Unless you have suddenly become incompetent at your job, I insist that they remain with you. I trust you."

Robert twisted his mouth. "With your *money* you do."

"Robert please..." she said, already exhausted with his unbending attitude.

"I'll keep your accounts. They require very little interaction except the yearly planning meeting."

"I *want* to have interaction with you. My god I'm sorry for overreacting, for not trusting you in *that* moment."

"You acted like I would purposely try to get you pregnant. While I *do* like your bank account, I've never tried to saddle a woman with a baby to get their money."

"You could have handled it better yourself, instead of reacting like I accused you of stealing the good china."

"Hell, that's what it felt like. The disdain you felt at the possibility of having a child with someone lowly like me, was clear by how badly you freaked out."

"Where in the world is all this coming from? Yes, I was horrified about the possibility of having *anyone's* child. This never had anything to do with your worth."

"It did to me!" Robert yelled pounding his desk with a fist. Only the nosy faces he saw openly looking into his office made him rein in his temper—but barely. Through gritted teeth and a lowered voice, he continued. "I told *you* I would always protect you—*us*—in that matter. I told *you* I had protected us that night and you looked me in the eye and said I was lying. Like I had no honor!"

"I freaked out! There I admit it. I'm a normal woman that sometimes has crazy emotions! Add in my PMS week and there you have it. I know, shocking that I'm more than *just* your fuck-buddy."

He stood up so quickly his chair flew behind him. "Get out. I think we're done having this conversation in my office." Robert was furious.

"I thought you believed in facing things head on?"

"You should leave before I have you shown out," he said coldly, straightening his suit and tie before putting his hands in his pockets.

Mika felt the back of her eyes sting. She had never attacked a man before but she thought about it now, *really* thought about it. She wanted to do something extreme and trifling, like the trashy shows she sometimes watched. Instead she channeled her inner Beverly, giving him a look of dismissal that would have done her mother proud. Turning on her heels and without another word, she walked out his office...and out of his life.

Chapter Twenty-One

It was the last weekend in February, and the last two weeks had been some of the roughest Mika could remember. To make matters worse, her cousins had been pestering her for a get together. With the mood she was in she didn't feel like talking to them. Every time she turned around one of them was calling, emailing, or texting her about picking a date for either lunch or dinner. So far she had put them off. Today was Saturday, and she was going to drown her sorrows, then watch some mindless TV.

She had just started on step one by pouring a big glass of wine. There was no one here to judge her but herself. God knows she had *way more* fucked-up things she could be judging herself for than being a weekend alcoholic. She had just put the bottle back in the fridge when her doorbell rang. Irrationally, she hoped it was Robert.

Leaving her wine, she shamelessly rushed to the door, but paused with her hand on the knob. Did she even want to talk to him right now? Some days she thought she did, other days she hoped he was somewhere rotting. Would they be able to have a civil conversation? She flung open the door then let out a pent up breath.

"This is exactly what I get for not using the peephole." Instead of slamming the door she just walked away.

"Well, hello to you too cousin...with your rude ass," Misha said as she walked in followed by Milissa and Michaelle.

"Whatever," Mika threw over her shoulder going back to retrieve her wine. With them here she was going to need it. When she came back to the living room, she found them all sitting down as if she had invited them.

"What do you guys want?" She asked still standing.

"The same thing we've wanted for the last week or so. To go out and eat," Lissa complained.

"I told you guys I didn't have time, I've been busy."

Michaelle slowly looked her up and down. "You don't look busy to me."

"Well I was about to be."

Misha got up nipping the wine glass from her cousin's hand, before taking a big sip.

"Go ahead and get dressed so we can go. We have a reservation at eleven-thirty. Nowhere fancy, just throw on something decent."

Mika huffed. Annoyed that her wine had been stolen along with their persistence in bothering her. "Look, I'm sorry you all came here for nothing. But I really can't go anywhere right now. I'm in a mood."

Lissa rolled her eyes. "Obviously."

"Enough already," Michaelle said standing up. Using the tone she had perfected in their youth to help control three younger girls when they were under her charge. "Go get dressed. You *are* going to lunch with your family." Giving Mika a little push she continued. "Hurry up, and we can get this over with."

"Fine, Y'all get on my nerves."

"Hurry along." Misha wiggled her fingers at her cousin's retreating form. "Let us know if *little* Mikala needs any help."

* * *

They went to Roses Restaurant & Lounge, which was right in Canton. A nice little Italian place she ordered take-out from. Honestly she was hungry and didn't mind eating here at all. After they were seated and water and bread was served, Mika turned to her family.

"So what do ya'll heffa's want with me so bad you had to track me down? I just saw you all two months ago."

"Who, you calling a heffa? None of us are fat cows, so I take exception to that," Lissa said blandly.

"Your m—" Misha started to say before Michaelle cut her off.

"Why do we need a reason to see you? There is no schedule of how many times we can talk per month or quarter," Michelle scolded.

"Well there *should* be," Mika mumbled.

"Tell us what you've been up to lately," Michaelle went on as if she hadn't heard her, while cutting her eyes at Misha who had a big mouth. If Mika found out they were here per her mother's request she wouldn't tell them anything. "How's your love life? Did you give Stanley a chance?"

"No, I've ignored all of Stanley's calls." Actually she had told him she was seriously dating someone else. Which had been true at the time.

"Ahh good! Does that mean you've found someone else? I was starting to worry. It's been a while since you mentioned anyone," Lissa said smiling.

When Mika remained silent Misha barely resisted the urge to shake her. "Mika, I swear if you don't stop acting like an ass I'm coming across this table—and *not* for a hug. You only get this weird over a guy you're really into, which doesn't happen that often. Tell us already. Maybe it will make you feel better."

They were slightly over a year apart in age, and because of this they tended to fuss at each other more often, even though they were the closest.

"I don't really know how I feel. Maybe it's for the best," Mika said on a sigh.

"Just tell us what's going on, and we'll be the judge," Michaelle said gently.

Mika proceeded to tell a quick summary of her and Robert's original fight, ending with the horrible confrontation in his office. By the time she had told it all, their lunch had arrived.

"Well," Michaelle finally said. "What company does he work for? I'm sure my husband can get him fired. He knows everybody."

Mika almost choked on her ice water. "Jeez, I don't want him to lose his job. He's my financial advisor and damn good at it."

All three cousins nodded their heads at that statement. After all money was business, some things you just never risked.

"Okay," Misha narrowed her eyes. "You said he works downtown right? My hubby knows some folks that can uh....teach him a lesson." When Mika just gaped at her she went on. "Okay fine, what city does he live in? I'm sure we can do it there. Give me his address."

Letting out a strangled laugh, Mika shook her head. "I admit I almost kicked his ass myself. I really thought about tossing him through that stupid glass wall in his office. But I don't want him hurt."

"You sure? It won't be traced back to us, I promise," Misha pushed.

"She said no," Lissa finally spoke up, an evil grin on her face. "She doesn't want him hurt. Guess she's a softie like that. I would gut the bastard. *Anyway* what about hurting his property? I mean there is a lot we could do! Do you know if he has a security system at his house?"

Mika was confused. All three cousins looked at her expectantly, waiting for the answer. They seemed to be dead serious about their suggestions. "I don't know if I should be creeped out or touched that you guys care so much."

Michaelle frowned. "Of course we do! It sounds like he really hurt you. We're not going to let him get away with doing that to our family."

"You've never seemed to care before. None of you take me seriously when I talk about what I'm looking for in a man."

"Here you go being dramatic. We *do* listen to you." Misha voice sounded tired. "All we do is *listen* as you constantly complain about your mother, or the perfectly acceptable men she tries to hook you up with."

"Oh please!" Mika was getting a little upset. "You guys never take up for me, always siding with her. I don't know why you just can't accept I'm not like the rest of you. I don't want respectability to be my only concern in life. I want to live life on my own terms, not some predetermined role someone else has for me. *If* I ever marry, I want to marry for love!"

There were several beats of silence—then Michaelle lit into her.

"You have always been a spoiled and somewhat selfish brat. It's because your mother couldn't have more kids and doted on you. Partly our fault as well, for putting up with your attitude over the years. We have *always* been on your side. We're your damn cousins. Hell we were practically raised as sisters!"

"And yes we agree with your mother and ours when you argue. Unlike you *we* learned the art of being subtle. You know...catching more bee's with honey and all that. We agree, as not to add fuel to the fire. When you leave we plead your case in a calmer manner."

Michaelle took a deep breath before she went on.

"And stop the bullshit about us accepting you *how you are*. Maybe you should start taking your own advice. You assume we—" She indicated herself and her sisters. "Are pretending to be something we're not. Did it occur to you this is just our personalities? That we *like* who we are and our lives!"

Mika was shrinking in her seat, but her oldest cousin wasn't done yet.

"And furthermore, you have always been so judgmental of us! How dare you insinuate we didn't marry for love? What you think, you the only black woman out here looking for a pot of gold at the end of the rainbow? If you didn't have *your* nose so stuck in the air you would have noticed our husbands don't treat us like trophy wives, but the queens that we are."

Michaelle leaned forward on the table. "*Our* mother and Aunt Beverly taught us what to expect from a man. Get over yourself! Since we were kids, *you're* the one who always pushed us away. We have always accepted you, just not the other way around."

When it was clear she had run out of steam and her tirade was done, not a word was said for a full ten seconds.

"I'm sorry. I never looked at how I came off from your point of view. I never took the time to look beyond the surface. I haven't taken the time to look at you all as full complex people. I'm sorry."

Mika took a long sip of her water fighting off the tightening of her throat. The number of people she was offending seemed to be climbing.

"I forgive you," Lissa said suddenly. "I looked up to you for a while growing up. You seemed so free and daring. I used to love when you would let me in on your adventures. Besides, we all talked once and decided you needed to paint us a certain way to make yourself feel superior." She shrugged her shoulders. "We figured we'd let you have it, since you couldn't seem to keep a man and all."

"Gee, thanks. And nice dig at the end."

Lissa grinned. "You're welcome!"

Mika turned to Misha. "You've been awfully quiet. Don't you have something to say?"

"Yeah, I do. I'm just trying to figure out how you thought we didn't like you, or didn't take up for you." Misha was genuinely confused and a little hurt. "When you were in school and refused to perm or hot comb your hair, who do you think defended you? Even though you stood out like a sore thumb?"

"Well, I stood up for myself. Honestly though I wasn't messed with that often about stuff like that. I was quirky by our bougie school standards, but folks seemed to accept it. Maybe I was just lucky."

"Luck, my ass." Misha snorted. "Michaelle and I wouldn't *allow* anyone to talk about you. We were fairly popular so that helped and for those that it didn't, we kicked their ass. We had your back all throughout school."

"What!" Mika sat in disbelief. "Come on you guys did not. You never got kicked out for fighting."

"Of course not that wouldn't have been proper now would it?" Michaelle slyly proclaimed. "Do you remember Stacey Higgins? You were in ninth grade, Misha was in tenth and I was a senior. Stacey was a year below me and she had always been a snot, you could tell she had a problem with black people. Anyway, you started school and she took to calling you the N-word. Saying how you didn't fit in because of your hair, and how you dressed more urban. You never told your parents and only told me because I found you crying in the bathroom. You told me she had been harassing you for months!"

Michaelle paused as indignation flooded her even after all these years. It had hurt her heart to see her cousin—who had always been bold, outgoing, and sure of herself, broken by an ugly racist word.

"I gave you that pep talk about rising above it, to ignore her and that you betta never let her see you cry. Never let her see her words affected you. That you were a queen and she was a peasant. For the next week I stalked her skinny ass and one day she went in the bathroom alone. I waited 'til she was washing her hands and hit her with a hard punch to her right kidney!"

They all gasped around the table, though Lissa's surprise quickly turned into a quiet chuckle.

"The little bitch dropped to one knee and I grabbed her ponytail. Told her if she *ever* called you or any other black person in that school the N-word again, I would beat her ass."

Michaelle had a reminiscing smile on her face. "I added that after I beat her ass, I'd have my *ghetto* cousins find her and they'd kick it again. Told her she betta not tell anyone either."

"But we don't have any hood cousins, at least none that live here," Lissa stated.

Michaelle rolled her eyes. "I know that, but *she* didn't. She probably thought all black families had thugs willing to beat people up. It must have worked as Mika never said she messed with her again."

Mika stared in awe at learning all this and had a new appreciation for her oldest cousin, who she had always thought was the stiffest of the bunch. "No, she never said another word to me. I kept hoping she would. I had newfound courage after you talked to me. Thank you...I didn't know."

"Good, and you're welcome. It's what family does."

"Yeah, the same way you did for me when I got to high school. We're family," Lissa said simply.

"We are, aren't we?" Mika started to cry. Everything with Robert and now this. It was all too much.

"Please stop, you're embarrassing yourself and *us*. Or at least do a pretty cry, you looking ugly," Misha quipped.

"Oh shut up!" Mika said but she was grinning and got her tears under control. "I'm sorry I didn't appreciate you guys more. I'll do better, I promise. You annoy me, but I love you all."

"We love you too, *Mikala*," Misha teased, as the waiter came over.

"Can we get a round of mimosas?" Michaelle addressed the server. "We just had a boatload of emotional family crap, and we need to fortify our nerves."

The cousins shared a laugh, but then Milissa turned to Mika. "Back to your original problem. You don't want to make him pay, so it sounds like you want to make up?"

Mika hesitated, but finally said. "Yeah, I guess. I definitely want to have a real conversation with him. I really thought we were in a good place before all this."

"Well what are you waiting on? He overreacted as well but only after you did. You know men and their egos," Misha reminded her.

"I know. Thanks for listening. It did help." Especially since she hadn't updated Andrea about the last argument or sought her advice. She still didn't feel right putting her in the middle of it.

Their drinks arrived and when everyone had a glass, Lissa asked. "What should we drink to?"

"To our dysfunctional and misunderstood family and hoping stupid men come to their senses," Mika warily said.

They all laughed and toasted though Mika noticed Milissa didn't actually take a sip. "What's with you? If you don't want yours I'll take it. I feel like I earned it, since I just found out I'm a major bitch."

Milissa eyes lit up and she flushed.

"I was looking forward to this meeting, for a reason of my own. I wanted to talk to you all about something."

"Well, spill it," Misha said,

"Okay. Brian and I are trying to get pregnant! We've only been trying for a month. It's early but I'd rather be cautious with the drinking. We don't know when it might take."

Amidst the congratulations and well wishes for Lissa to conceive soon, Mika saw the joy on her cousin's face at the hope of expanding her family. She felt her heart melt. Right then she came to the conclusion that she *did* in fact want kids. She wanted to plan having kids with a husband, anticipating a new life to love. Not right away, but one day.

Chapter Twenty-Two

As the first Wednesday in March rolled in, nothing much had changed. Lunch with her cousins may have enlightened her about her family, but it hadn't done anything to clarify her love life. She wanted to fix things with Robert or at least try. She just didn't know how to go about it. He could be so obstinate. When she thought back to their confrontation in his office, it was like she hadn't known the man in front of her. Had they been at a strong enough place in their budding relationship to overcome this? She had decided she wanted to try, but did he?

Now to make matters worse, Robert's sister had emailed wanting to meet for lunch. Why she had agreed was the real question. Probably because she liked Brihanna, and felt they shouldn't be deprived of getting to know each other. Had he even told any of his family they were dating? She had no clue, and that was a problem in itself. Up until recently their relationship had been so casual, they had barely gotten serious before this stupid fight.

Mika supposed it didn't matter if Brihanna knew about them or not, seeing as technically they were over. She looked at her wall clock and saw it was ten minutes to noon. They were supposed to be meeting in the lobby soon. Imagine her disbelief as she watched a co-worker bring a grimacing Brihanna to her office.

Brihanna thanked the woman for her help, before walking in and shutting the door. Mika took note that she was in a pair of faded jeans. The bottom of a blue plaid shirt showed from under her short leather coat, which was trimmed at the neck and wrists with black fur. Mika liked that she pulled it all together with some heeled ankle boots that were also fur lined. The only other color Brihanna had on was some blue stud earrings which were only visible because she had her long hair pulled into a ponytail.

"I thought we were meeting downstairs."

"Yeah." Brihanna dropped down in a chair. "About that, I figured I'd save some time and just come up here. Hopefully this won't take up much time for either of us."

Mika sighed, it looked like her March was going to be just as confrontational as her February. "Say what you got to say."

Brihanna narrowed her eyes leaning forward, before flopping back. "What did you do to my brother?" Brihanna said sullenly.

"How do you know your brother didn't do something to *me*?"

"Okay, fair point. What happened?"

"You should ask your brother," Mika deflected. "I'm pretty sure he wouldn't want me telling his business."

"I *did* ask. He's been in such a foul mood for the last few weeks, snapping my head off left and right. I asked if something happened between you two and he told me to 'mind my own damn business', then basically threw me out his house."

Shocked Mika asked the younger woman, "You know about us?"

Brihanna rolled her eyes. "Don't be naive. I grilled him a couple of days after Thanksgiving and found out you guys were hooking-up. He even told me you entered a more real relationship at the start of the year."

Mika's eyebrows rose. "He said we were in a real relationship?"

"Of course he didn't use *those* words." Brihanna rolled her eyes in the other direction. "He said you guys were officially dating instead of merely doing the bump and grind."

"He did *not* say that to you!" Mika laughed despite the situation.

Brihanna let a small smile curve her lips. "Okay, I added that last part." Losing her smile as quickly as it had come she suddenly popped up and started pacing the office. "What happened? He's been *super* happy since January. In general he's been more laid back ever since you started bumping nasties way back when—though I guess *anyone* getting sex on the regular would be."

Mika waved her hand to stop the other woman's rambling. "Please sit down. You making my head hurt between your pacing and talking a million miles an hour."

Mika watched as Brihanna suddenly stopped, dropping back down as if her strings had been cut. The girl looked so dejected that it made Mika feel worse. "Look, I just don't feel right talking to you about this if he won't."

Brihanna waved her hand dismissively. "Come on you know men. They clam up when they get hurt, and I think he's really hurting right now. Look whatever he did, unless it was cheating which I don't think he'd do. My brother is brutally honest. He would just break up with you before banging someone else."

"Anyone ever tell you that you have a way with words when it comes to describing sex?"

"I was raised with boys so I'm a little blunt and crass. It drives my mother and aunt crazy." Brihanna smirked before frowning. "I was saying unless it was *really* bad you should give him another chance. I think he really likes you. I've never seen him like this...well not since he was a teenager. Men are stupid and stubborn. Maybe if you went to him...reached out first."

"I did." Mika was suddenly tired. "I apologized for my part of it, but he wasn't trying to hear it. When that didn't work I went to him in person...tried to talk. The only thing that accomplished was us having a bigger and nastier fight."

Mika voice cracked on the next words. "I don't know what else to do! Your brother can be cold as ice. Sometimes...I don't even know if I want to be with someone capable of acting that way."

Brihanna sighed. "He's only like that when he feels threatened. I swear he's really a teddy bear. He's the best brother I could ever ask for, he practically raised me. It's because of him we're all stable and thriving. He takes care of everyone emotionally too. Like a mother hen making sure all his little "chicks" are in place and where they should be. We're five years apart but we're super close if you couldn't tell."

Mika cracked a smile, rapidly blinking to keep her eyes from leaking. "Yeah, I got a clue when you walked in here to confront me."

"I'm not sorry I did. My brother has taken care of me my whole life. I know firsthand how much love he has to give. When he accepts someone into his circle he protects them, cares for them." Brihanna shrugged. "But he's also slow to trust, slow to open up. He reacts badly when he's hurt or deeply disappointed. I was so excited he'd found a woman who shook him up a bit. That he actually seemed to like, you know on a deeper level."

"It's sweet that you care so much. I just don't know what to tell you. I don't know if we can fix it." Mika bit her lip but said it anyway, "I'll admit, I want to give it a try. It's just...we can both be a little closed-off. It takes *two* people to want to make up."

"I know. He's used to being a 'when he's done, he's done' type person."

"So am I," Mika said. "Ironic huh?"

"Well this time I don't think he can be. He normally just moves on. Right now he's mopey, moody and restless, all at the same time. You got under his skin."

Brihanna stood up and pulled her gloves out of her pockets. "I'll push him some more on being less pigheaded, if you'll hang in there a little bit longer until he comes to his senses. Do we have a deal?"

Brihanna held out her hand and after a moment of hesitation, Mika stood up and shook it. "You have a deal."

"Good! I think you'll both regret it if you don't give this another shot. You seem just as miserable as he is."

"Well that's comforting," Mika mumbled sarcastically as she went and opened the door.

"It *should* be. It means you both care about the other. Thanks for the time. I really hope I'll be seeing you around."

Mika watched as Brihanna took quick, confident strides down the hall towards the elevators. While Robert was high-class business fashion, his sister was more casual with a chic punk lean to her style. Still, the two had a lot in common. Both had no regrets when they took bold or impulsive actions. And they both seemed to like making deals as well. She liked Brihanna, and hoped she would get to know the woman better.

* * *

Robert was pissed at himself for still being in a funk over *that woman*. He couldn't bring himself to think of her directly. To many memories assaulted him and made it all worse. Even the best liquor in his house couldn't quiet his mind when it came to her. Though he made sure not to hit the bottle *too* hard, he needed to be clear-headed. He'd already made a number of bad decisions, starting from when he'd gone to her house way back in October. He'd known then she would be trouble, following his dick instead of his head, now look at him.

While he wasn't snapping at anyone at work, they were avoiding him like the angry black man he currently was. He didn't speak unless he had to, and when he did his communication was short and curt. Antonio had been the only one with enough balls to ask him if he was okay. He'd replied with the universal statement that all men around the world understood, "Women, who needs them right?" His friend had looked at him in barely concealed pity, readily agreeing before taking him out for a lunchtime drink.

Outside of work was a different story, no one was safe. He'd been avoiding his mother for a good two weeks. She had that mother's intuition when things were going south. He couldn't stand to be around his cousins for long either. Even Cam had tried to talk to him twice about the situation and promptly got checked to stay out of it. The man had eased off in the last week, maybe he'd realized there was nothing to talk about when it came to Mika.

Dealing with Brihanna was a whole other matter. His sister was a bit too much like him sometimes, and she wasn't afraid of pushing him like everyone else was. She and Mika had that in common. Brihanna usually dropped by once a week or called, and he'd been lashing out at her since this whole thing started. Three days ago, when she'd brought him some take-out he tried brushing off her company.

When she had connected his bad mood to Mika he'd lost his shit. He'd told her to get the hell out if she couldn't stay out of his business and respect his privacy. The look of shock and hurt on her face had made him feel like crap. Before he could work his mouth around to apologizing, she had packed up the food and left. Shouting that he would end up a shriveled, old lonely man if he kept pushing people away.

Was he doing that? Pushing people away? Probably. Just like he was brutally honest with others, he *tried* to be just as honest with himself. He knew he was acting like a wounded animal that wanted to hide in a cave until it was healed. He admitted—at least to himself that he was hurting. More than he thought was possible for a woman he'd only known for roughly six months.

She had struck a hard blow to his ego, and more importantly to his honor. The latter was something that was dear to him going back to his childhood. He had grown up quick after his father left his mother with a newborn. At five his carefree childhood had changed, as he tried his best to help his stressed out mother and comfort a fussy baby. Being so young himself he couldn't help much, but he'd fetched bags, bottles, diapers, or sung to entertain Brihanna.

What he *had* been able to do was change his behavior. Almost overnight he'd become a quiet watchful child. A little boy's natural wildness, tempered by his natural empathy for the two women in his life. By the time he was eight his mother was working two jobs and he learned to cook. Simple things like sandwiches, oatmeal, spaghetti, and a number of other easy dishes. His mother was often tired but she spent what little time she had left helping him with homework, filling in the educational gaps of the Detroit public school system. She was a big part of why he'd taken education so seriously and why he'd gotten several scholarships. Those had allowed him to go to the expensive University of Michigan.

Of course his mom had help from Aunt Dolores. Robert spent half his time at her house when he was young, surrounded by his cousins. It was there he could relax, let go and just be a kid. He loved spending time at Aunt D's house, horsing around with Devon and Darrell, the three of them following behind Thomas and Edward. While the two older boys alternately ignored them or got them in trouble with their schemes.

When he turned twelve his mom allowed them to stay home by themselves more often. Some years she had three jobs, picking up part-time holiday work. All to keep a roof over their heads, clothes on their backs, and food in their mouths. He'd decided then that he wanted a stable life when he was an adult. Excitement wasn't all it was cracked up to be. He preferred having money so he wouldn't have to cry and pray about how to pay the bills like his mother had.

That sparked his interest to learn everything about money he could. How to get it, how to keep it, and all the ways to make it. He'd wanted to be able to take care of his mother and aunt as soon as he could. Even before he attended college he was great at saving and had started some tentative investments with the help of a teacher. By the time he had reached his sophomore year in college he was passing on his knowledge to the rest of his immediate family. He taught them how to budget better and save. How to do more long-term planning and invest.

He'd helped guide his older cousins to maximize the incomes they had to sustain their growing households. Since he and Thomas were the oldest they were seen as the "rocks" of both families. Well on the male side at least. His mother and Aunt Dolores were the true foundations, and always would be. Their strength of raising six kids on the west side of Detroit, all of which had survived the streets to become productive citizens, deserved that crown.

His family looked to him as a fixer of any problems that arose. It was in his DNA to take care of those he cared about. So it had felt like a stab to the chest, when Mika thought he hadn't protected her. That he'd purposely cosign her to the uncertainty of being a single mother. The salt in his wound was when she accused him of lying on top of everything else.

As if he would ever downplay something as serious as a child? Did she think he would deny his own kid? He would have taken care of his child and been in their life if a pregnancy had resulted. Did she think so little of him? These types of thoughts rotated through his mind and infuriated him. Her actions told him she didn't trust him enough...he was *not* his father! He wouldn't run when shit got real and responsibility came knocking on his door. He hadn't at five years old, and he wouldn't at thirty-two.

His upbringing was the reason he was always hesitant to commit to any woman. When you made promises there was the potential of breaking them. He had dreaded when mama got her hopes up, only to be disappointed again. He never wanted to see the disappointment and hope drain out his own kid's eyes, as it had for him and Brihanna. His father's blood ran in his veins and he worried about those traits coming to the forefront. He refused to be a lazy coward, wasting his potential or talent. Letting down the people who needed and loved him the most. As an adult he kept his circle small. It was probably best Mika was no longer in it.

Robert shook off all his depressing thoughts, rising to go fix himself another drink. It was Thursday night, one more day left to get through the work week. He'd been bringing more and more work home so his mind didn't conjure up a curly-haired diva with a mischievous smile. Thinking of mischievous women he needed to make up with his sister too. There had been silence from her end which was unusual as Brihanna didn't know how to take no for an answer or tolerate losing any better than he did.

He picked up his phone intending to give her a call while it was on his mind, and saw a text he'd missed.

Mama: I'm going to call you in a few minutes and you're going to pick up that phone Robert Lorde. Don't make me call twice!

Robert grimaced. His mother rarely texted him, preferring the old school method of talking on the phone. When his phone rang less than a minute later he picked it up even though it was the last thing he wanted to do right now.

"Hey, Mama. Is everything okay?"

"Does something have to be wrong for a mother to talk to her only son?"

"I guess not, since we're talking," he said with dry amusement.

"Don't get smart with me. I'm not in the mood for it after you've been dodging me for weeks. What's going on with you? Are you okay?"

"I'm fine Ma. You know you don't have to worry about me."

"Son, I'm your mother. I'll *always* worry about you. Now please tell me what's going on...talk to me."

After a long pause he decided he might as well. They'd always been open and honest with each other. Their family unit of three had always been that way. They were all they had. Trust, communication, and working together had been essential to survive. He gave her a quick rundown of his and Mika's relationship, such as it was. Then he shared everything that had happened over Valentine's Day weekend. When he was finished, his mother didn't say anything for a while, just a couple of "hmm's", as was her habit when she was thinking.

"I'm sorry to hear this happened. She seemed like a lovely woman actually. I liked her spirit. Are you sure you can't work this out? She *did* apologize for overreacting and handling the situation poorly."

"Handling the situation poorly is an understatement. Mama she basically accused me of purposely forgetting the condom, which I didn't at all. Didn't believe me either when I told her I'd worn one! Like I was some trifling-ass man who didn't give a damn about her or myself. She didn't trust me to protect her!"

"Son a woman *wants* to believe in a man...but the reality is we never know." Johanna sighed heavily. "The consequences for *us* can be severe. You think I thought your daddy was gon up and leave me with two kids? And *we* were married! I chose him thinking he was ready for marriage, for kids. He damn sure was there when we were making them."

Johanna paused to let that sink in. "I know it's not fair but try to look at it from her view. Ya'll are barely dating, just a few months ago at Thanksgiving you were calling her a friend when you clearly were more. She freaked out, and I can't say I blame her. But if she apologized and realized her mistake...well just think about it. Try not to let your hard head lead you away from your heart."

"My heart has nothing to do with it. It's about who I am as a man. She clearly doesn't know me or respect me."

"Oh Robert, you're still lying to yourself. Your heart has *everything* to do with it. I know it can hurt to put yourself out there. But *you* taught us all that without any risk, there can be no reward."

Chapter Twenty-Three

While Mika was thankful it was Friday quitting time couldn't come fast enough! Everyone at work was getting on her nerves! It was only noon but she decided to get out the office for lunch though food wasn't really on her mind. Mika had lost her appetite, something that had never happened before over a man. So instead of picking up food she was just walking, occasionally looking into storefronts. Walking past a flower shop she stopped dead in her tracks, as the name on the window got her attention. This was the shop Robert got her flowers from. She went inside before she could think better of it.

"Is there something I can help you with or would you like to look around?" A pretty black woman asked looking up from the bouquet she was making.

"I'll look around for a bit."

"No problem...take your time." The clerk went right back to working on her arrangement.

Mika was already distracted as well, making her way through the surprisingly large store, looking at various flowers and gifts. Recognizing some of the flowers invoked a lot of memories. She had never figured out why Robert sent the odd number of flowers. Though she had actually liked that they were never the normal dozen or half-dozen. The uniqueness of wondering what she would get at the beginning of most work weeks had been exciting. She took her time browsing and didn't know how long it had been before a voice made her jump.

"Sorry about the wait. I'm Yolanda, is there anything I can help you find?"

"No, not really. I don't even know why I'm in here."

"Oh it's okay, sometimes it's hard to focus after you've lost a loved one. But we can do anything you can think of."

Was she giving out depression vibes *that* strong that the lady thought someone had died? Although losing a boyfriend, man-friend, sex-buddy—hell *whatever* he had been might count. "No one died.'"

The clerk smiled relieved. "Glad to hear it! Were you looking for anything in particular?"

"I'm sorry, I don't even know why I came in. A friend used to send me flowers from here all the time. They were always so beautiful. When I walked by and noticed the shop I decided to come in."

"That's excellent! I love it when our work makes an impression! Do you mind sharing your name? Maybe I'll remember one of the arrangements. I do a big bulk of them."

"My name is Mika, but I doubt you'll remember. I'm sure you do so many." When the woman's mouth dropped Mika could tell she was wrong.

"Oh my goodness, you're *the* Mika!" The woman looked her up and down several times. Mika decided not to take offense since she was grinning as she did it. "You work for an ad agency right?"

"Yes that's me." This was getting a little weird.

"Rhonda won't believe I met you! Girl congrats on having such a dedicated and romantic man! Where did you find him? And are there two more like him for me and my cousin?"

Mika laughed, shaking her head. "He's not my man. And he's not romantic. You sure you got the right guy?"

"Oh honey, I'm sure." Yolanda fanned herself before continuing. "Over six feet, dressed to the nines. Dark chocolate with an intense businessman vibe about him. Full sexy lips—"

"Okay, okay. That sounds like Robert." Mika rushed to cut the woman off before the weirdness reared up another notch.

"Yes! Robert Lorde! Even the name makes you want to drop your panties!"

"I get it." Where had the professional shop owner gone? "But just because he orders flowers that you put together for him, doesn't make him romantic." Why was she trying to burst this woman's bubble? Why was she still in this store? And why was this woman looking at her like *she* was the messed up one?

"We put them together yes, but we never decided what went out. Most of the time that fine-ass man—excuse my language—walked into the store and picked out each flower himself."

"He what?"

"You heard me. He'd come in early in the morning, and I got to admit seeing him was better than a cup of coffee to get me going! Only thing we did was arrange, wrap and deliver them."

"That doesn't sound like something he'd do," Mika mumbled more to herself than the lady.

"Well, he did. As owners we would have preferred he get the normal dozen or half-dozen. I even asked him the first two times to just give us a budget and we'd put something nice together for him but he refused. No offense, but he said the flowers were for a woman who was very picky, so he had to get it just right."

"Now *that* sounds like something he'd say."

"All I know is men who normally come inside are trying to "make up" for something. They just want us to put together an arrangement *quickly*. They don't take time to hand-select *anything*. Tell me how you snagged a man like that? This is so inappropriate but I'm thirty-five and will take any tips I can get. What kind of *voodoo do you do* in the bedroom to get that man hooked?"

"Excuse me!" Even as Mika said it she cringed because she sounded as snooty as her mother.

Looking around to make sure they remained alone, the clerk continued. "You don't have to be shy we're grown adults. Look I know about the *reason* he gives you such odd numbers of flowers, mixing up the variety."

"You do?"

"Yes, and don't worry he was a gentleman. We kept asking him why he picked your flowers out the way he did. He answered one day when he was kinda distracted. Saying they were an expression of the time he spent with you. That each flower represented a *moment* between you two. Now like I said he wasn't crass about it, but he had the kind of satisfied half-smile on his face that didn't make me think he was just talking about dates."

While Mika felt her jaw go slack, she watched the woman's expression go soft and dreamy.

"Sometimes he would call the store in advance and request a specialty flower. Those are harder to come by blooms that our customers can pay a premium for as we get them from a larger florist."

Mika felt her throat tighten. "I didn't know any of this."

"It's so rare to find a man like that." Yolanda turned her head as the store bell tinkled announcing another customer. "I got a kick out of meeting you! I'm going to go help this customer but please let me know if you need anything. I'll give you a 30% discount since your man spends so much with us."

Mika slipped out the door as soon as the clerk got busy. She spent the rest of the workday in a daze and the drive home was no different. Once home her mind kept running over what she had learned, trying to make it fit into the

Robert she *thought* she knew. She ate dinner but didn't taste a thing. After taking her shower early and getting into bedclothes, she laid down on the couch and turned on a random show. Her mind focused on processing everything from Brihanna to the flower shop bombshell. Robert apparently had other sides to him. A protector and helper to his family, and a closet romantic who handpicked flowers. Filled with symbolism and meaning, while putting his personal touch on each arrangement. On her walk back to work she had looked up the meaning of a yellow Chrysanthemum. One of the meanings symbolized neglected love and sorrow...the last flower he'd sent her after their fight.

When she thought back she realized he'd done a dozen little things to show her he really cared about her. Like always putting her car up in his garage, so she didn't have to deal with the weather. Even doing things out of his comfort zone, like taking her to the zoo and talking to the girls at the center.

Robert wasn't a grand gesture kind of guy, which was probably why she liked him. With him you knew that when he *did* make a kind or sweet gesture, he *meant* it. He wasn't a bull-shitter, didn't do things for appearances' sake or even to spare someone's feelings. He was truthful and direct. He would have never lied to her about that condom, even if a mistake had been made.

She groaned in misery. Her own stupidity and fear had set this whole thing in motion. Rolling from the couch to the floor she slowly sat up before grabbing her phone. She called the one person who could help her make sense of everything.

* * *

Andrea was just coming down the steps when her cell rang. She saw it was Mika and hurriedly answered. "Hey."

Her bestie had been tight-lipped since her breakup and Andrea was ecstatic she was reaching out.

"Hey," Mika replied softly.

Andrea allowed the silence on the phone to last a few beats before asking, "What can I do?"

"Can you come over?"

"Give me forty-five," Andrea said immediately.

"Thank you."

"No thanks needed, that's what I'm here for."

Andrea hung up and went to the kitchen where Cam was making a sandwich. "Hey, I'm going over to Mika's, not sure what time I'll be back."

Stopping what he was doing, he went to give her a quick kiss. "No problem. Just text me when you're on your way home. Let me know if you need anything."

"Will do."

"Give her my love."

Andrea hugged him. "No can do. I keep your love just for me. Call me selfish."

"I like it! My baby *possessive!*" He gave her a soft tap on the behind. "You're turning me on. You betta get out of here before you get detained."

Chapter Twenty-Four

Andrea had stayed for over three hours last night, not going home until close to midnight. Mika had filled her in on everything since she'd last seen her. Andrea felt all of Robert's behavior showed that he cared about her and was even falling in love; he just didn't know how to say it out loud. When it came to the flowers Andrea had gotten the same sappy look in her eye as the clerk. It just so happened Mika had kept a picture of every arrangement he'd ever sent her, guess she was sappy as well. The two had combed the internet for the meanings of each flower as Mika thought back on their time together before each arrival, it all added up.

He had been expressing his feelings the whole time. Slowly but surely his feelings had been getting stronger. She had been ill-equipped to see it, being as she hadn't known what genuine affection looked like. Mika was used to men seeing her body, wanting to hang out just for fun, either in or outside the bedroom.

She had cried a little, then a lot after that inner revelation. Andrea offering her hugs and wine. The latter of which she had declined and Andrea had promptly declared her either ill or in love. As the night went on Andrea said she believed Robert would come around as he was obviously missing her, per Brihanna's report. Andrea also pointed out how Robert had *pursued* her all this time. How he basically initiated every date or face-to-face interaction they'd had. Mika had been surprised that this had never dawned on her before.

Her friend felt a man like Robert who never chased women, had to care an awful lot to put himself out there like he had with her. That he was sensible to a fault and would calm down and try to sort this out. Mika wasn't so sure of that, reminding Andrea how he'd treated her in his office. Andrea had waved that away, saying men could be more vindictive and hold grudges longer than women. Just look at how "easygoing" Cam had frozen her out completely for months!

That reminder had shifted the conversation to Andrea's tales of married life. Mika allowed her stories to distract her and make her laugh. It actually made her feel better to see how in love and happy her best friend was. It sparked a little ember of hope in her own heart. When Andrea was leaving she gave me an extra-hard hug and the same advice I'd given her—not to wait too long before making it right. Although she followed that up by saying she had a feeling Robert would be gracing my doorstep soon.

Now it was Saturday the next day and Mika felt more clearheaded. It was around three in the afternoon as she was worked up the courage to call Robert. Pacing up and down the hallway with the phone in her hand. Eventually her legs carried her to the kitchen.

"Maybe I'll have a *small* glass of wine first."

She poured a nice smooth red and continued pacing, this time in the kitchen. She knew she was stalling. In the past a big argument with a man meant she deleted their number and never saw them again. So this uncomfortable situation of trying to work through issues was foreign to her. Just as her finger was about to bring his number up, she heard her bell ring.

"Ugh...I'm not expecting anyone." She quickly did a mental check to see if she had any packages arriving, but concluded she hadn't ordered anything in a while. Pulling up her security app that allowed her to see who was outside, she almost dropped the phone. It was Robert!

"Damn!" Calling him was one thing but she wasn't prepared for the man in the flesh. She watched as he rang the bell again, this time looking up at the camera that he knew was there, raising that arrogant eyebrow of his.

Robert knew she was looking at him through the peephole or through the camera that she'd made him install after the last time he'd randomly shown up. After the conversation with his mother and a tirade from Brihanna when he called to apologize, he had sat down and really evaluated their entire relationship. Pushing his hurt and anger aside, to look at it from an objective 360-view.

Their relationship had always been a tightrope walk for them both. Neither of them had been confident in the direction they were heading, as they tried to navigate the landmines of a "real relationship". From when they'd started as "wary combatants" then headed to "hesitant lovers", and finally arrived at the "new couple" stage. They'd come a long way when he thought about it.

His mother was right, his heart was involved. He'd known that really from the start but had brushed it off as treating her differently due to the bond they had with their friends. No the truth was all this was new for him, and he hadn't wanted to put a name to what he was feeling. That would make it "real".

The way he had treated her had zero to do with Cam and Andrea. It may have started with him wanting to get in her pants, morphing into him wanting to make her happy, and in the end just be around her. He felt good when she was near, even at the start when they were needling each other. Her vibe gave him life, energized him. Robert had known her strong fear of getting pregnant and instead of being coolheaded and relieving her panic, his ego had added to it. Afterward, he'd only made it worse by refusing her apology. A man was supposed to soothe and vanquish his woman's fears and problems, not *be* the problem. He was hoping he could make it right. He didn't want to lose someone he had just figured out he needed in his life.

When the door finally opened, he swept his eyes over her, drinking in the sight. "Can I come in?"

"I think that's the first time you've ever asked."

Robert gave a small smile. "Is that a yes? You never answer my questions."

"You might as well. I literally was about to call you." She wiggled the phone still cradled in her hand.

"That's good." He entered and watched as she shut the door. "That means we're thinking along the same lines."

"That remains to be seen. Let's have a seat, my feet are tired from pacing." She led him into the living room, her heart beating a mile a minute as he sat on the couch angling towards her. Her first instinct was to hug him, touch him and punch him all at the same time.

They sat looking at each other until he finally said, "You look good...but you always do."

"Is that all you came here to say Robert?"

"Naw." He rubbed a hand over the top of his head before leaning forward. "I'm stalling, just like you were with the pacing."

She briefly touched his leg. "I'm glad you're here...I think it's important we talk."

The woman had only touched him for two seconds, yet he felt the tingle through his clothes. That's how in-tune his body was to hers. He gritted his teeth to remain focused and just came out with it.

"I'm sorry, about the way I acted that morning. I could have cleared everything up right then." When she went to interrupt he shook his head. "I'm sorry that I didn't accept your apology. It took a lot to admit you had overreacted, and I was petty not to let it go. I'm sorry that I wasn't secure enough to talk when you came to my office trying to move past it. In a nutshell I was wrong. I want us to move on from this, if it's something you want as well."

Mika didn't know what she'd expected. The reality of him admitting his part in the disaster was refreshing. The day had come when Robert Lorde had apologized readily and fully, it was a new day indeed! He was quietly waiting on her response, not pushing or rushing just waiting. Still strong, still full of pride, yet vulnerable as he looked in her eyes. She reached out and took his hand.

"I want that as well. Thank you for the apology. I'll give you mine again. I'm sorry for how I reacted." She squeezed his hand. "I *know* the man who remembers each and *every* time we've been intimate and celebrates it with flowers, is a man I can trust."

Robert let out a half embarrassed laugh. "You finally figured it out huh?"

"Yeah, with a little help from your biggest fan, Yolanda at the flower shop." Mika couldn't help it. The cute bashful smile on his face made her lean in and give him a quick peck on the lips.

"I knew I could trust you *before* I found out how sappy and romantic you are. I'm so sorry I ever made you think I didn't. What I've never been sure of, was exactly where we stood with each other." She lifted their combined hands in example.

"Let's call a spade a spade." Robert announced. "We're in a relationship."

"Are we?"

He sighed heavily. Damn women for always wanting the words. "It's what I'd like, and what we've been building up to. Do people who aren't in a relationship have a fight like we just did? Unless they genuinely care for each other?"

"Some do."

"Well, *I* don't. I want us to acknowledge we're a couple in a full-fledged, serious relationship. No more grey area."

"Okay," she said quickly, suddenly shy. Mika bit her lip hard struggling not to shout out she was falling in love with him. Things were suddenly moving fast, she didn't want to complicate things further. One step at a time was probably best for them.

"I guess I'm in *like* with you," she said slyly, scooting closer and putting her arms around his back.

"Just *like*? You sure?" He gave her ass a gentle squeeze.

She nodded her head yes before asking, "If I were to give you a note asking if you liked *me*, would you check yes or no?"

He threw his head back laughing. "Neither. I'd ball it up then do this," He swooped forward and kissed her until she went limp. "That would be *part* of the answer."

"And what would the other part be?"

"I'd take your face in my hands." He did. "Look you in your eyes...and tell you I'm falling in love with you." He saw her eyes get watery but she didn't say anything, while his heart knocked in his chest. "Hopefully in that scenario you won't leave me hanging."

"I wouldn't leave you hanging." She let out a nervous laugh, her voice wavering. "You caught me off guard. I was *just* thinking I didn't want to say the same and scare you off."

She stroked his jaw, palming his face. "I'm falling in love with you too. I think we're in for a helluva ride."

Chapter Twenty-Five

As spring rolled in their relationship grew, just like the budding flowers. From March on they spent large amounts of time together. Their communication skyrocketing as well. The new couple spent endless time talking with each other on the phone, through text, email, and in person. Filling in the gaps of knowledge they didn't already know about each other.

Whenever there was *any* question of a comment or action done by the other, they just asked for clarity. They worked to not let their defensiveness of these new feelings and situations get the best of them, and overall it worked. Simply put they were a full-fledged couple who were very happy. Their friends sighed with relief at the news and the four of them had gone on several double-dates since.

By April, Mika's neighbors were waving hello to Robert as they all started on their yardwork. One Saturday Mika's mother had done a rare but not unheard of drop by. Robert had answered the door with an open shirt and jeans slung low on his hips. Her mother had been taken aback as Mika came upon the two. Beverly stayed long enough to have a cup of coffee and a chat with them. As her mother was leaving she had given Mika a hug, followed by a thumbs-up and a wink. Her mother apparently approved of her choice in romantic partner.

Then one night in late April, after a date where she ended up at his place they *made love*. It wasn't the first time since their reconciliation, but something about this time felt different. They trailed their hands along skin, kissed softly but deeply, admired and revered each other's bodies. Appreciation and satisfaction there in each other's eyes at the pleasure they were giving the other. Finished they had lain facing each other when Mika said what was in her heart.

"Hey stalker...guess what?"
"I'm not a stalker." He kissed her forehead. "What?"
"You are a stalker. But I love you...anyway."
"You love me?" Robert said faintly until the words sunk in. He half-sat up. "You love me?"
"Yes. I love you Robert Lorde, even with all your horrible faults." She smiled but then got serious and stroked his face. "I love you."
He put his forehead against hers. "I love you too. You're my annoying princess, but God help me I love you."

It was now late May and Robert had gotten them tickets to a Tigers game. He had sprung for seats on the lower level directly behind the dugout. Excellent seats! They had gone to Opening Day last month, but she was excited to take in another game, as they were having outstanding weather lately.

Mika was in her orange Tigers shirt with her foam Tigers paw, thoroughly enjoying the game. Robert found all her hand props for sports to be ridiculous. He had laughed and taken her picture next to the huge tiger at the gate anyway. As they were coming into the seventh inning stretch, she was busy nibbling on his ear. He kept pushing her away and telling her to focus on the game.

"Ugh, fine. Then go get me a hotdog," she said to him.

"You can wait until the vender comes back around."

"Why can't you do it? The break just started." Mika looked at him and noticed he was fidgeting.

"Just watch the game Mika," Robert said tensely.

She threw up her hands, shifting in her seat. "He's telling me to watch the game and they're not even playing," Mika mumbled to herself.

She glanced at the field, then at the monitors. Sometimes there were interesting baseball tidbits that she didn't know. After the first trivia question flashed on the screen, she thought about complaining for her hotdog again, when she saw:

MIKA WILL YOU MARRY ME? R.L.

She snapped her head around so fast she was sure whiplash would follow tomorrow. Robert brought out the box he'd been hiding in his hand and opened it, while she looked at him wide-eyed. He was sweating, and it had nothing to do with the sunny day.

"Mikala Renee Harrison, will you marry me?"

"Oh my god, yes! Yes!"

It was too fast, crazy and it was perfect! Throwing her arms around him their lips met for a joyful kiss. On the screen their faces were shown before fireworks graphics replaced them. The crowd around them continued to cheer. Mika was stupefied that he'd asked, and Robert was in disbelief *and* relief she'd said yes!

Pulling back, Robert slipped the ring on her finger and she squealed, getting her first real look at it. He had to physically tilt her head up to regain her attention.

"You sure about this...even though I'm not your type." Robert inquired eyes serious and questioning.

"I'm positive. You are not my type to date, but you're my perfect type to marry." Mika gave him an impassioned kiss, putting all that she felt into it. Pulling Robert up by the hand she grabbed her stuff as well. "Let's get out of here. I can show you at home just *how* much my type you *really* are."

* * *

They didn't end up going home but instead made a stop not far from the stadium. When Cam answered the door he gave them an easy smile and ushered them in.

"Is Andrea home?" Mika was impatiently bouncing on her toes.

"Yeah, she's here." Yelling towards the stairs, "Andrea come on down! Mika is here!"

Andrea didn't respond but they heard her footsteps soon enough. "Hey you two! I see you took in a game. How was it?"

"It was the best game ever! Look what I got!" Mika held up her hand and wiggled her fingers.

There was a heartbeat of silence as Andrea's eyes took a second to send the message of what she was seeing to her brain. Then she let out a shriek, which triggered a shriek from Mika and the two women ran at each other.

Both men winced, and Cam quickly moved away from the screeching and jumping women over to Robert, giving him a man hug and a hard pat on the back.

"This is happening huh?" Cam had a huge smile on his face.

Robert rubbed his brow and grinned back. "Yeah, it is."

"You do remember being in this *very* house, telling me I was proposing too soon, a couple months shy of a year after I met Andrea."

"Yeah...I might remember something like that," Robert said slowly.

"Yet, it's only been eight months and *you* popped the question. Didn't I tell you! When it's the right one, you just know!"

"You told me. I guess somethings you have to learn for yourself. I see the light now." They shared a laugh and another hug.

Meanwhile a few feet away, the ladies had settled down enough to actually talk.

"I can't believe this!" Andrea breathed out, trying to catch her breath.

"Me either! He had them put the proposal on the big screen. Must have cost him a pretty penny." Mika let out a wild laugh. "I know he hated that but it's more proof that he loves me."

"Aww, that is romantic! Now let me really look at this ring!" Andrea gripped Mika's hand bringing it closer.

Robert had gotten her a 2 carat diamond with a ruby nestled on either side. Along the sides of the white-gold band were two rows of inset diamonds. So that the entire thing sparkled, no matter which way you looked at it.

"It's beautiful!" Andrea let out her own laugh. "This *so* fits you, you can see this from across a room!"

"Girl, I know! I asked what made him decide on this ring. He said he needed something that was colorful, that blazed and dazzled like I do. Robert waxing poetic! I almost made him pull over so I could jump him!"

Robert walked over and pulled Mika back to him. "What did I hear about jumping my bones? We can get out of here and take care of that."

"*That* can wait, you're going to have the rest of your lives for that. Give me a hug." Andrea pushed Mika out the way embracing Robert. "I can't believe you proposed!"

"Hey!" Mika objected.

"It's okay," Cam consoled her. "You can hug Mr. Sexy."

Mika did as he congratulated her. "You *are* Mr. Sexy. But I'm marrying Tall, Dark, and Handsome!"

The two couples traded places before Andrea asked, "Have you thought about when yet?"

Cam looked down at his wife. "Dang, they just got engaged."

"Yes, sometime in the fall I'm thinking," Mika said almost at the same time. "I'll have firmer ideas after Robert and I talk it out."

"You sure you want to wait that long before you tie the knot?" Cam teased. "I don't want him to change his mind, though I'll help you track him down if he bolts."

"He won't if he knows what's good for him." Mika elbowed Robert, who just rolled his eyes.

"Ya'll tripping. I make sound decisions that I stick by." He turned to his future wife, giving her a look that was just for her. "Mika is a solid investment. She will drive me crazy, but I expect to get a boatload of dividends back well into old age."

Chapter Twenty-Six

By the time they left Andrea's house, it was around four in the afternoon and Mika knew her parents should be at home. Sometimes her father liked to golf, but that would have ended hours ago. She was so excited that she didn't bother knocking, using her emergency key instead. Quickly deactivating the alarm and calling out. "Mama, Daddy, are you home?"

The pair were already walking towards the entrance. Her mother came toward her clutching her chest.

"What's wrong? What's happened?" Beverly rushed her questions out. Mika never used her key just because. Even when they were expecting her she rang the doorbell. The girl rarely called her "Mama" either.

"What's the problem babygirl?" Reginald aimed a glare at the man standing by his Mika's side. A couple of months may have passed, but he hadn't yet forgiven the man completely for hurting his little girl's feelings. Word had come from the cousins to his wife, then from his wife to him.

"Nothing is wrong. I'm sorry Mika barged in like this and scared you both." That earned Robert a swat on the shoulder as Mika turned on him.

"Hey, don't apologizing for me."

"*Someone* had to do it. You could have waited until they answered the door."

As much as it usually amused Beverly to see someone going toe-to-toe with her stubborn daughter, she was still uncertain *what* was going on. "Can you both please save your display for later and explain what in the world is going on?"

"Sorry, you're right." Turning her blinding smile on her parents Mika announced, "Robert asked me to marry him and I said yes. I'm getting married!" She launched herself at both parents.

Beverly accepted the hug before pushing her daughter back, looking into her sparkling eyes. The unadulterated happiness she saw in them held her tongue. She wanted to question whether it was too soon, whether she was sure, and whether they were both ready. Instead she gave Mikala a hard hug back. "That's wonderful! Let me see the ring!"

Reginald walked forward and held out his hand to Robert. "Congratulations son. You better make my little girl happy."

"It will be top on my to-do list for the rest of my life."

"He will." Mika turned to Robert, giving him a slow smile. "He takes extremely good care of the women he cares about." Going to her father she gave him another hug. "I can't wait for you to walk me down the aisle."

"Of course sweetheart. Whatever you want for your wedding, you'll have. Anything, just name it and it's yours."

"We can't let you do that Daddy. It's not the 1800s. Robert and I can pay for the wedding."

Robert cleared his throat loudly, getting everyone's attention. "As I'm the financial advisor for both of us, I'm going to have to disagree. I'm all in favor of your father paying. If he wants to gift his *only* daughter with her dream wedding who are we to take that from him?"

Mika's mother's loud snort of laughter followed that comment. She was full-out laughing looking over at the love of her own life. "Well, at least we know they'll never be broke the way he watches those coins."

"I'll give him points for that. Watching coins is how a person ends up with dollar bills."

Now it was Robert's turn to grin. "Exactly right Sir."

Reginald slapped him on the back. "Come on let's all celebrate!"

The four enjoyed a celebratory toast before the couple left. At some point her father had taken Robert off to have a short, "man-to-man" talk. While her mother had pressed her for wedding ideas, even though she had only gotten engaged mere hours ago.

* * *

They drove to see his mother who lived in Southfield after leaving her parents' house. Robert called first to make sure Johanna was home and ask if he could drop by. Always happy to see her son, she told him to come on over.

Mika gripped Robert's hand tightly as they walked up the walkway. She had met his mother a total of two times now, having had dinner with her and Brihanna since their reconciliation. The woman seemed warm, outgoing and classy. She also absolutely loved her kids. Mika hoped she didn't have that odd clinginess that bordered on possessiveness, which so many mothers of only sons had. This phenomenon seemed to run especially deep in black households.

Would she be happy for them, knowing she now had to share Robert? It was easy to see Robert adored both his mother and sister, he spoiled them. People said you could tell how a man would treat his wife, by how he treated his mother and female relatives. Which is why she had no doubt that he would treat her like the queen she was. Now if she could just make sure his mother and sister were firmly apart of her royal court.

"Hey honey!" Johanna greeted both of them. "Why didn't you tell me you were bringing Mika! Come on in!"

215

"Sorry Mama." Robert gave her a big kiss on the cheek. They were ushered into the living room, where she had two cups of coffee ready. "Mika do you want a cup of coffee or something else? I have tea, water, and some juice."

"Definitely not any coffee ma'am, I'm already jittery."

"I noticed." Johanna wrinkled her brow. "You okay? Let me go get you some tea."

"Mama," Robert interrupted before she could leave the room. "I asked Mika to be my wife, and she accepted."

"Oh!" Johanna let out the stunned sound, before covering her mouth as her eyes started to water. "Oh, my goodness!" She cried this time in excitement. She rushed over to her son and envelop him. "I'm so happy for you! Both of you!" She said, switching to take Mika in a bear hug.

She finally pulled back holding Mika hands. "I knew it! I knew the look in my baby's eye when he saw you standing in that kitchen on Thanksgiving. You had his attention! Robert's focus is a powerful thing and when a man looks at a woman like *that,* and it blocks out everything else in the room...well I knew he had met his match!"

"Thank you. I'm very happy to be joining your family."

Johanna snorted. "Ha! I'm glad we getting *you.* Now I'll have another sane person around."

Robert twisted his mouth. "She's not sane...she's a State alum and fanatic."

"Oh." Johanna's voice said it all, before she gave Mika's hand a pat. "I guess everyone has issues. Now let me see this ring!"

* * *

The next month was spent brainstorming and planning the basics: the when, what, and where. After hashing it out with Robert and then her mother, Mika settled on a small destination wedding. The guests would be mostly family, and a few friends. Her father was happy to pay for the venue once she picked it, plus the flight and accommodations for the wedding party.

Robert surprised the rest of his immediate family not directly in the wedding, by paying their way as well. While they could easily pay themselves he volunteered to dip into his savings for it—which Mika found out was *way above* what her bank accounts were holding. Guess being generally cheap *did* pay off.

When Darrell had heard about his generosity, he teased his cousin by saying, "Man, she must be breaking you off something nice to have *your* cheap ass willingly coughing up dough."

Robert had just shook his head and laughed, socking Darrell hard in the arm later when he least expected it.

The wedding party would consist of:

Andrea-Matron of Honor	Camden-Best Man
Brihanna-Bridesmaid	Devon-Groomsman
Misha-Bridesmaid	Darrell-Groomsman
Michaelle-Bridesmaid	Edward-Groomsman
Kimberly-Bridesmaid	Thomas-Groomsman
Julia-Bridesmaid	Antonio-Groomsman

The ring bearer would be Michaelle's young son, who Mika hoped would be up to the job, as he wouldn't be *quite* three years old yet. The flower girl would be Edward's youngest daughter. Milissa was opting out since she would be five and a half months pregnant. Mika had told her she didn't care, but Lissa refused to be her definition of "fat", especially while everyone else looked great in their dresses. Since it evened out the wedding party Mika hadn't pushed.

With both of their families including Andrea's parents, who thought of Mika like another daughter, the entire wedding would be about 33 people. Her mother convinced them to invite five more people for a more *pleasing* even number.

Mika had rolled her eyes but gone for it. Robert did have one aunt on his father's side that he liked, so he invited her and her husband. Mika had rounded out the last three with an older distant great Aunt who was loaded and liked to travel with her spouse. The last was a friend she had met at her first job after college. The sista worked in her field and they kept in fairly close contact, often helping each other with difficult work issues. Bringing the grand number of people who would be at this wedding to 38.

The wedding would take place during the Thanksgiving weekend. Most people already had that weekend off, and everyone seemed happy to leave the Michigan cold for the holiday. They would arrive early on Thursday and celebrate Turkey Day, with the rehearsal and dinner the next day on Friday. They would get married on Saturday evening, and guests could fly home on Sunday. With plenty of time for some relaxation between wedding duties.

She and Robert would spend another three days there after the ceremony before moving on to their second honeymoon location in Bali. A romantic and sightseeing paradise. She had gone back and forth on the actual wedding location. However being with Robert was rubbing off on her, so she decided on the cheaper option of Jamaica instead of the Bahamas. Plus she felt folks knew how to party more in Jamaica and she definitely wanted this to be a hype occasion.

Once the basics were decided they spent the next four and a half months taking care of the details. She and the girls negotiated over the style of the bridesmaids' dresses, while she controlled the color. Her mother handled the floral arrangements, some of which would need to be imported. Luckily, they were able to find several great bakers on the island for the cake.

As each month ticked by they made it happen, checking off various details. Between Andrea, her mother and Aunt Jackie, shit got done. All three had the organizational skills of generals—especially with her daddy's pocketbook in the background picking up any slack. Her wacky vision of her special day coming into realization. The cherry on top was that she was *in* love *and was* loved back.

Chapter Twenty-Seven

They were in Montego Bay, Jamaica! The main group touched down before noon on Thanksgiving Day. By two, they were taking elaborate photos with the wedding party. Between her and Andrea's work connections and her dad's poor wallet, they'd hired a well-known professional who lived on the island but was making a name for himself in the States as well. Somehow that didn't stop Lissa from trying to direct him from the sidelines as Mika had insisted she be in a few shots per location. The man showed great restraint as far as Mika was concerned. They had three wardrobe changes because *yes* she was going to be extra, she only planned on getting married once.

The swimsuit session was done on the beach, in the water and on a boat. The women had one-piece and bikini sets in wedding colors, while she allowed the men to wear a tank and shorts but insisted they do a few shots topless. They didn't know it but she planned to make a calendar for the group to start the year off and she figured the ladies should have equal amount of eye candy up on their walls.

The next was evening wear. Pictures had been taken on the grand steps of the resort's entrance, and along its marble halls. Mika rocked the dress Robert had bought her, while her ladies wore white. When his eyes landed on her lighting up, she felt like a sensual vixen. He had been right *this* dress did her justice. Locking eyes, Mika knew they were both thinking about how the first dress had been destroyed.

The photographer showed them a few preview shots saying they were smoking hot. Which was hard to dispute seeing how she and Robert touched and kissed in-between *and* during takes. So much so their friends told them to get a room. They took the suggestion when the photographer moved to the wedding party pictures, disappearing to a bathroom around the corner. No dresses were torn this time, but the quickie was just as intense and passionate.

After a quick change, the group traveled to nearby Martha Brae River Nature Park to do casualwear. They took group and individual pictures in the park section before Mika and Robert did some balancing acts on a bamboo raft as they floated down the river. The photographer on a raft behind them directing their poses. The backdrop along their route was amazing, and they took photos laying in each other's arms and with their legs dipped in the water as they gazed into each other's eyes.

They didn't get back to the hotel until around seven, which was a little later than planned. Which left them with only an hour before T-Day dinner with the rest of the family. They were all exhausted, but the entire group had been very accommodating. Robert hadn't complained or rushed her once and never hesitated to try any position she or the photographer wanted. Even *after* he had taken ribbing from his younger cousins over the more romantic and mushy ones.

Dinner went well as they filled everyone in on how the shots had gone, sharing a few photos of the backdrops via their phones. It was a fun and lively dinner, and Mika was surprised at how relaxed her mother and aunt were around Robert's family. They'd had dinner with everyone a few months back and it had been a much stiffer affair on both sides. But today there was nothing but laughter, jokes, and all-around good vibes as they gave thanks for the blessings in their lives. Only Darrell got drunk, though quite a few people would have joined him with just another drink or two. The group called it a night by ten. Everyone needed some rest and recovery from jet lag and the exhausting day.

Friday dawned and Beverly made Mika and Andrea get up early, checking all the details for tomorrow. All things thankfully seemed to be in order. The cake was on schedule and the flowers were beautiful. There was one change with the menu, as they needed to swap out a side dish. Beverly and the chef agreed on an acceptable substitution without much fuss before finalizing everything.

After lunch she and Robert surprised everyone with a spa day to relax and de-stress. Everyone got two services of their choice, and the use of the steam room. They had a handful of hours before the rehearsal and dinner, so folks broke off in groups or went off alone to rest or sightsee. Mika and Robert went on a Catamaran ride with Cam and Andrea so they could get away from it all. It felt good to have some alone time with their core group. The ease in which they all interacted and understood each other was a special thing that was relaxing all on its own.

The ceremony rehearsal started at six, and the group marched down to the skeleton of a tent that had been put up. The final set-up and decorations would be done early the following day. The onsite wedding planner walked them through where the guests would be and where the front of the makeshift altar was. Moving on to the actual process of the ceremony, including where the wedding party would stand, along with the groom and bride final positions.

Finally it was time to actually rehearse. The first time ended in jokes and laughter, as they got things a little confused. The second time around was much better, as everyone focused. The officiator then ran though the order of what would be said with Mika and Robert. When Mika started to cry everyone panicked, including Robert.

"Nothing is wrong," Mika assured them. "I'm just getting all my crying out the way now. Someone told me I cry ugly and I can't have that in my wedding pictures, now can I?"

Everyone let out a relieved laugh and Misha shot her a grin. Mika only rolled her eyes and grinned back at her. They wrapped up around seven and went inside for the catered rehearsal dinner. At first she had been almost too nervous to eat. She was getting married in less than 24 hours! It didn't seem real, yet here they were. Andrea urged her to eat since she was nervously drinking wine. That got her reluctantly lifting her fork. The only thing she wanted to be drunk on tonight was love.

Once again there was lots of laughter, pictures being taken, jokes and even toasts. As the dinner came to a close Cam stood up to give his own.

"Can I have everyone's attention before we go?" Once he had it he continued. "This toast is very special to me for several reasons, and it's to the beautiful bride."

Mika looked right then left, pointing to herself mouthing, "Me?" Before grinning. "Yes you, the one and only. I've been meaning to give you a gift for over two years. Ever since you pushed Andrea into my arms, which was the best blessing of my life. You've done many things to support our relationship. I want you and Robert to know we plan to do the same for you both. We love you and want you to be happy. If the bride could come up here."

Robert helped her stand before they walked up front, hanging back as Mika went to Cam's side. He knew Cam had a soft spot for Mika, and this was their moment.

"I want to give you this bracelet as a token of *my* affection." Cam pulled a seven and a half inch white-gold bracelet from his pocket. Made by tiny hearts connecting together. Spaced evenly around it were four sterling silver, heart-shaped charms. Cam hooked it around her left wrist and continued.

"The first charm says *friend*, as you've been a friend to me from the start. The second is *sister*, what you are to my wife. The third says *bold, bright woman*. Mika your light shines brightly on those around you. The last says *lover, friend, wife*. What you are and will become for my brother tomorrow."

The crowd aww'd and clapped.

Mika could see a few other women in the crowd with leaky eyes and wiped away a single tear from her own. "Sexy Cam this is so beautiful!" She gave him a big hug before stepping back.

"Trouble, this doesn't come close to what I owe you for helping me and Robert discover love. You'll not find a harder working, determined, or more honorable man than Robert. Except maybe me, and I'm taken. *Thank you,* and I wish you both nothing but love!"

Hugs were given all around among the friends, before Andrea made an announcement. "Okay people, let's keep the celebration going! The best man and I are going to steal all the ladies and gentlemen for a surprise bachelor and bachelorette party!

* * *

Andrea and Cam had worked hard to keep this part a secret. She'd had to go behind Beverly's back with the venue planner to pull off her and Cam's plans. This was directly out of their own pockets. The two had wanted to treat not only the bride and groom, but everyone else that had given up their normal Thanksgiving plans to take part in the event. The youngest kids were put to bed, and the older kids and teens were tasked with watching them from their connected room. Andrea had also arranged for resort staff to check in on the kids until they knew the family had returned.

After changing into party clothes, every adult met downstairs in the lobby by 9:30. Once everyone arrived Andrea and Cam led the two sexes in opposite directions to private spaces. Both rooms were loosely decorated like Vegas bars, replicating where the couple had first partied with each other. Mika absolutely loved it! Andrea put a crown on her head and a big, bold pin on her chest that said "Bride". The room shared a toast first, and then the real party began.

The DJ started with some oldies but goodies that had even the older ladies all dancing. It helped that sexy men were walking around—some dressed fully, others not so much—who danced and interacted with them.

Mika spied Aunt Dolores fanning herself and pushing Johanna directly in the arms of a shirtless and muscled young man who couldn't have been older than thirty. Johanna seemed horrified, but Mika gave Dolores a thumbs-up from across the room. She really liked that woman! She decided to do the same to her mother. Bringing over two men and sandwiching Beverly Harrison dead in the middle. Her mother stopped dancing and narrowed her eyes at Mika, before flipping her hair and going right back to swaying those hips. Mika's mouth dropped while her Aunt Jackie pushed her out the way laughing, deciding to join in the fun with her sister.

Mika stood there with her cousins, as they all stared in fascination at their stuffy mothers getting down.

"Only you Mikala could make this happen. These are the kind of sights you can't get out of your head...ever," Misha said.

"Agreed, I'll need to increase my therapy sessions after this," Michaelle said. "Someone had to have spiked their drinks. That will be the thought that comforts me."

"I think it's hilarious!" Lissa hollered over the music. "Why are we standing here letting these old women outdo us? Let's go dance!"

And they did: drinking, dancing, laughing and using the photo booth to take stupid pictures. Andrea had banned any other photos, so the women could let loose. A few tables were set up and when they got tired they sat and talked or ate the appetizers that came out midway through the hour. Andrea made sure that all the men danced or flirted with Mika—though she needn't have made the effort. Jamaican men enjoyed flirting with beautiful women. No woman in the room was neglected.

Mika pulled Andrea aside later on. "Sis thank you so much for this. This was so perfect! Thank you for everything! I know between me and my mother we've driven you a little crazy."

Andrea waved away her thanks. "I'm used to you. And don't hit me but you're more like your mother than you think." Mika hit her. "Ouch! Anyway, I'm having a great time too, and so is everyone else. Besides friends 'til the end! Wait...that sounds a little creepy, like the Chucky doll."

They laughed but Mika nodded her head. "It *does* sound creepy, but it's true. Friends forever!"

They shared a hard hug before Andrea pulled back. "The night's not over yet. I have one last surprise for you!"

Chapter Twenty-Eight

Meanwhile in the men's room they drank, and some even smoked cigars. A stage had been set up for dancers to do routines for the men, while a few women mingled dancing with them or talking. Most had on skimpy showgirl outfits to go with the room's theme, while others had on sexy tight dresses with crazy high heels. Black women of all hues, thick, thin and in-between; Robert was sure there was something for every man's taste in the room. Before they had entered Cam had draped a V-shaped sash around him that hung like a necklace, hitting his upper chest. On the end there was a large button that said "Groom".

In the corner was a screened off portion of the room, where he *believed* private lap dances were happening. He didn't plan on finding out for sure. But he didn't think it was a coincidence there was an ATM located right outside the door. Cam had made it clear no camera use was allowed, and that what happened in this room stayed here. For folks to keep it as clean as *their* conscious could tolerate and have fun.

Robert figured it would be fine. Most of the men were married—or in front of their fathers-in-law. As long as the money was for regular old-fashioned lap dances and no "extras", everyone would be good. Besides he wasn't here to police people. He just knew *he* didn't plan to ruin his marriage before it started. Plus he never forgot that his future wife could likely kick his ass. Trying not to think about what was going on in *her* room, he relaxed and enjoyed the evening.

He flirted and danced, all while keeping his hands in the proper places. His eyes soaking up all the curves and booty-shaking they could. He was getting married but he wasn't dead. Throughout the night it seemed like everyone, while in various states of being buzzed or drunk—pulled him aside to give him advice or a talking to. Mika's father had finally threatened him, "you treat my daughter right or I'll kill you", using those exact words. Then he'd smiled, clapping him so hard on the back Robert stumbled forward spilling his drink. Soon after her uncle by marriage had done the same thing, but in a much nicer way.

Then the husbands of Mika's cousins had surrounded him. He'd come to know them a bit and liked them well enough. Enough so he wouldn't feel put out when he had to spend family gatherings with them. He liked their various connections even better. He listened to their take on joining "the family". That they were nowhere near as stuffy as the front they put on in public, which Robert had already figured out for himself.

Her mother was easy to deal with, compliment her and agree on little things. Mrs. Harrison was by no means fooled that he was a pliable or easy man, but she liked that he respected her, and responded with the same accord to him. Mika's father was by nature an easygoing and friendly man. However, when they talked about business it was easy to see how astute he was. How he'd risen so high at a time when a black man barely could get his toe inside corporate boardrooms, much less a full seat at the table. Robert admired the man. Plus, once Reginald saw that his wife had accepted Robert fully *and* that his daughter was happy, well that was all the man cared about. Robert planned to follow the man's example of "happy wife, happy life". Though after the honeymoon he really needed to talk to his father-in-law about ways to recoup some of the money the man had shelled out for this wedding.

Darrell and Devon had dragged him off together and asked him for the tenth time if he was ready for this? And for the tenth time he'd told them he was, or he wouldn't have proposed. They'd nodded patting him on the back, and told him not to fuck it up before walking off. He'd barely taken a few steps before his two older cousins cornered him with words of advice. Edward giving him tips on how to stay married, while Thomas gave him tips on what signs to look for, that might signal issues down the road. He respectfully listened to his cousins, then pushed them both in the direction of two women who were waiting for dance partners.

Even Earl, Andrea's father had snagged him. Telling him that a man put his wife and family first above all things. Never take the small things a woman did to make her man feel comfortable or tended to for granted. His advice sounded logical to Robert, so he filed it away. When Antonio caught up with him his only words of advice were "good luck". Then he thanked him again for letting him be a part of the big day. Robert waved his thanks off, encouraging him to go have some fun.

Later he'd been standing by the bar sipping a fresh scotch when Cam came over.

"You good?"

Robert nodded. "Yeah, just taking it all in." He set his drink down. "This is dope. I appreciate it."

"My pleasure. Had to do it big for the *fall* of Robert Lorde." Cam chuckled.

"Ha-ha. Laugh it up. Tomorrow we'll both be officially whipped and married men."

"Tomorrow?" Cam took a sip of his own drink. "Shit, we both whipped *today.*" Cam laughed outright, long and hard. He was buzzed, but made sure he stayed at that level so he could oversee the festivities. "Mika got your ass dangling your feet in rivers while holding hands, can't get more whipped than that."

Cam dodged the right jab Robert aimed his way and just smiled at the middle finger he got instead. Feeling his phone vibrate in his pocket, he checked and saw it was Andrea saying he had fifteen minutes. Smiling he looked back over at Robert.

"I need to take care of the next surprise in store for you."

Robert frowned. "I'm good. This is great. I don't need another surprise." He had thoroughly enjoyed himself since arriving on the island. But he was tired and really just wanted Mika and a bed...in that order.

"Trust, I got you. This surprise you'll love," Cam promised and walked off.

Mika had been blindfolded and sat off to the side. What the hell was going on? She heard Andrea gathering all the other ladies—before she heard whispering, then loud laughs and giggles. Andrea came back and stood her up, walking her who knows where.

"Where are we going?"

"Just out in the hall."

"And *why* am I blindfolded?"

"You'll know in a minute. Now hush and stop asking questions." Andrea said right before Mika was lifted high by three sets of strong, manly hands.

"Make sure you don't drop her! She *has* to walk down the aisle tomorrow!" Her mother called out as they started down the hall.

"Thanks," Mika said dryly. "What about telling them to put me down?"

"Hush, and hold still so they don't drop you," was Beverly's only reply.

Mika complied as she was carried on, silence around her except for the twittering of the women following the procession. There was no music or anything else she could hear as the men finally lowered her down.

"Okay, now what?" Mika asked.

"Now," Andrea answered. "You need to do one last crazy thing before you get married. You're going to give a little private lap-dance to a man here tonight."

Mika frowned and shook her head, "Umm, I don't think so. My future husband reacts badly to other men touching me."

"I *know*, that's why I blindfolded you. You'll have plausible deniability if it ever comes up, which it won't. Don't worry it's just a dance, the guy will keep his hands to himself."

"I don't know..."

"Come on don't tell me he has you tethered *already*," Misha goaded Mika, a sure way to get her to do most things. "What happened to the Mika who wouldn't have thought twice about dancing up on a man? Remember Essence Fest? When we were in the middle of Bourbon Street and you—"

"Okay, okay. You keep quiet." Mika aimed a glare in the general direction of her cousin. "Fine, point me in the direction of this guy and get me some music going."

Robert had watched as Cam cleared the room of all the women, the DJ remained but turned down the music. Then Cam placed a chair in the middle of the floor telling Robert to sit, before dragging everyone else off to the corner. Robert had no clue what was said but when they returned there were smiles and chuckles. When Cam pulled out a cloth and tried to put it around his mouth, he'd had enough.

"Naw, you not putting no damn gag on me."

233

Cam saw Robert wasn't going to bend, "Okay, I didn't really think you would. But swear that you'll be quiet, no matter what you see in the next few minutes."

"Just *what* will I be seeing?" Robert asked instead.

"Just promise on your future wife you'll sit down and shut up for five damn minutes."

"Okay, five minutes." Robert gave him that much then watched as Cam sent off a quick text before giving the DJ a signal to cut the music.

He sat relaxed, until three half-naked men carried Mika into the room, like she was Nefertiti. He glared at Cam who just smiled and silently reminded him to be quiet. Robert felt better when they lowered her and left. Listening he heard her conversation with Andrea and Misha, as all the men in the room remained completely quiet.

He watched, devouring Mika as she was led over to him. She was looking hot and sexy, wearing a sequined emerald colored party dress cut diagonally at the hem. The short side only reaching mid-thigh, the longer side barely hitting her knees. Dangling diamonds hung from her ears, his ruby and diamond ring glittering on her finger. She looked stunning. He wasn't surprised she was willing to give a dance to some man she couldn't even see. He *was* shocked they'd had to talk her into it. So he stayed silent as Mika stepped between his spread thighs and the music came back on with a slow sensual song.

Mika stood between some stranger's thighs and sighed. Why had she ever thought crazy stuff like this was fun? When she heard flashes going off she whipped her head around. "Are some of you traitors taking pictures?"

"Sure am," Lissa said without an ounce of apology in her voice. "You never know when I'll need to blackmail you into babysitting."

Mika bit her tongue. She had a policy of not talking bad about pregnant women, not wanting to curse her own children down the road. So she turned back around to the man in front of her. The sooner she got this over with, the better. She took another step forward and it brought her up against the hard bulge in his pants. Jeezus...she was going to kill Andrea, or whoever the hell came up with this prank. Reaching out her hands met a pair of shoulders and she followed them up a strong neck, then to an even stronger jaw.

Mika slowly smiled before backing up just a little, proceeding to sway her hips to the beat of the song, undulating her body side to side. She kept her movements fairly small, since it was easy to become unbalanced while not being able to see. After a while, she got into it, her girlfriends cheering and egging her own. She forgot there was a crowd watching and performed for herself and the man in front of her. Gliding her hands down her chest and hips, before turning her back and bracing her hands on his knees, bending at the waist to shake her ass in his face.

Carefully turning back around, she walked forward until she could feel his hardness once again. Mika had to admit she felt wild and free—just the way she loved to be! Starting high on his chest she moved both hands slowly down the firm surface. Squatting between his knees before running her hands down the sides of his stomach, crisscrossing until her hands landed on firm thighs. She gripped them, rubbing the length before retracing her journey back up. Mika traced the man's face again, following his jawline to his chin, then lips. Using her fingers as a guide, she quickly leaned forward to nip at the man's bottom lip.

Robert decided he deserved a medal for staying silent as he watched Mika put a temptress smile on her face and start dancing. He reminded himself it was just a dance, that she had a right to bachelorette-party antics. His rational thoughts lasted until she turned around and bent her ass in his face. The cut of the dress leaving nothing to the imagination. But when she turned around and brushed his penis again before caressing him, he was torn between being incredibly turned on and pissed that she would do this to another man.

So when she bit his *lip*—the room erupted and so did he!

The noise of the others faded and the DJ suddenly cut the song. Robert snapped his arms around Mika, pulling her onto his lap. "Really? You kissing on some random man?" Robert growled at her.

Mika only smiled laughing low, "You idiot, I knew as soon as I felt your shoulders not to mention that conceited jaw of yours. I know my man when I feel him." Mika tore the blindfold off as she talked.

Her response calmed down the crowd and more *importantly* her fiancé.

"Good. Because I'd hate to have to hurt a man on foreign soil," Robert chided, standing up but not letting her go. He ignored the comments, teasing, and camera flashes from their friends and family, only addressing Mika. "Playtime is over Princess."

Saying so he lifted her over a broad shoulder and started walking toward the door. Mika was happily hanging over his back, smiling ear to ear, waving at everyone even as she blushed.

"Wait a minute! You can't drag her out of here like this...before the wedding!" Mika's mother spluttered after the pair.

"Watch me," Robert said to the hoots and hollers left in his wake.

Chapter Twenty-Nine

It was another beautiful island day as Saturday arrived for the wedding. The party from last night had continued after Robert had stolen the bride. The dance and subsequent abduction had been scandalous, however no one watching could deny the passion and underlying love the couple had for each other. So husbands and wives reconnected that night, dancing, talking and flirting. Any desire they'd briefly had for the entertainers redirected to their significant others. It was almost a given that every couple had gotten lucky that night.

That didn't stop Mika's mother from getting up and checking on things before noon. Thankfully, everything was on track, and she texted as much to Andrea. Mika shouldn't have to deal with anything today except tying the knot. The Matron of Honor was up and about well before she got Beverly's message. Currently she was on her way to make sure the other few guests had made it to the resort. Once they got checked in, Andrea gave them a rundown of the timeline for the day, then left them to relax and rest. Andrea then went to make sure all the rest of the female wedding party had everything they needed.

Mika was sitting in a hairdresser's chair by three-thirty. Andrea had snatched her up from Robert's room a little over an hour ago. The two had spent a glorious night together, which left Mika wondering how in the world the honeymoon would beat it? The satisfied couple had slept late, both needing the rest. Having had breakfast in bed as they ignored the few texts and phone calls they received—until Andrea came banging on the door to retrieve her.

Mika was completely relaxed. Amazing sex along with family and friends who were taking care of all the details would do that to a girl. Her mother forwarded a picture of the finished cake and Mika was thrilled with the result! Their colors were green and blue, representing their respective schools. The cake reflected this too. It was a fairly traditional five-layer, white wedding cake. Classic decorative designs in blue were woven around it, and green flowers snaked up the towers on either side to meet at the top.

Her mother had been surprised she wanted such a simple cake, but Mika was saving the "wow" factor for the cake toppers. Custom made dolls molded to look exactly like her and Robert graced the top. The doll maker had outfitted her doppelganger in a green and white wedding dress, with an S on the chest. Even the doll's hair was exactly like hers! Robert's replica was dressed in a blue tux with an M in maize across the middle. Both of them had thought it would be a funny and a cute keepsake.

The ceremony was on the beach, however they would be using portable fake floors, specifically designed for sitting on top of sand. Making it easier for dancing and walking. Mika would be in low heels, and everyone else in sandals. Her dress was a short green, sleeveless cocktail dress that had a sheer, glittery, shark-bite sheath which flowed over her, almost like a veil. Her mother had been appalled that she wasn't wearing white. The only thing white would be the flowers in her hand and the white-gold bracelet recently given to her. She had started to straighten her hair but Robert liked it best when it was curly. She had settled on a front up-do that allowed her face to be prominent, yet still allowed her hair to be big in the back.

Her ladies in waiting would have on white, long flowing summer dresses that had green panels of material within it.

Robert and his crew would have azure-blue summer suits with small touches of maize in their ties and handkerchiefs. The tent would be littered inside and out with only the various flowers that Robert had sent her during their courtship. This event was wholly unique and fully their own.

By four-fifteen the wedding party resided in the two large dressing tents, set near the main wedding site, one each for the men and women. Mika was pumped! With their dresses being simple, it made getting ready easy. Most were just adding on the finishing touches like makeup and jewelry. While the other women fretted and ran around Mika was relaxing and chilling. Just waiting for the wedding planner to signal that it was time to start. As four-thirty hit everything calmed down, and the chatter went from nervous energy to excitement—except for her mother who was walking a hole in the fake floor.

"Mama, would you sit down, you're making me dizzy. Everything has been done and taken care of. Unless there is a sudden sinkhole the wedding will go off without a hitch."

"I'm not worried about the preparations. I'm worried about you!" Beverly clutched the pearls at her neck worrying her lip with her teeth.

Mika sighed heavily, rising to take her mother's hand. "Let's go have some *girl talk* time." Mika took her out the tent so they could talk in private.

"Why are you worried about me? I'm fine. I'm getting married, I'm on cloud nine!"

"That's just it, most brides *are* nervous. I'm worried you're not taking this seriously enough! Marriage should be *forever* Mikala. Not a game or a whim, or an activity you try for a while."

Mika took a deep breath and thought about where her mother was coming from, before assuming she was purposely trying to be negative. She had seen how hard her mother worked these last few months to make the wedding of Mika's dreams come true. Beverly was viewing her through a mother's eye, seeing Mika's need to do a little bit of everything as indecision, her willingness to jump without looking as impulsiveness. The truth was her mother didn't understand how being creative and doing new things, brought her daughter joy and excitement. However just because she didn't understand, didn't mean she didn't love her.

"I know you just want the best for me, for me to be happy. I realize that now. And I'm sorry I didn't always appreciate how you tried to protect me, from the things *you* thought would hurt me."

"I certainly do. You're my only child, my shining star. I want you to have a good solid marriage like your father and I. Someone you can grow old with, start a family...when you're ready. A husband to love and support you—and before you start I'm not talking about money." Beverly gave her daughter a searching look. "A blind person can see you have sexual chemistry up the wazoo. But do you have a love that runs as deep?"

"You can rest easy mama. My love for Robert is deeper than I thought I could *ever* love a man. I know it seems sudden but Robert is the ying to my yang. I've never felt as safe as I do with him. He loves me in the skin I'm in, and I love him just the way he is too."

Mika took her mother's hand again. "I know you don't know him well yet. But if you did, you'd know Robert takes everything super-seriously. He is *not* a fly by the seat of your pants type of man. He grounds me, and I help him fly every once in a while. He would not have asked me to marry him if he wasn't sure, he doesn't say things he doesn't mean. That's why when he asked, I said yes. I love him Mother, and he loves me. We're both ready and *that's* why I'm not nervous. I'm just excited and ready to start the rest of our lives."

Beverly squeezed her baby's hand. "That's what I needed to hear. Okay, I'm so happy and sad at the same time. But that's just how parents feel at weddings. Let's go get you married!"

Mika gave her a kiss before pushing her towards the tent. "Go on inside and give me five minutes, I'll be right behind you."

Once her mother was gone she inhaled deeply taking in the fresh air. Mika thought about how much of her life she'd judged her mother outward stances, instead of looking at the actions towards her as love, same with her cousins. Yet here she was marrying a man that she had instantly been attracted to, but disliked on sight. She realized she had done what so many men did to *her*. Judged him by his outward appearance only. She was so thankful fate had thrown them together again and couldn't wait to become his wife!

* * *

Meanwhile over in the men's tent, Robert was super quiet as the rest of the guys joked and fooled around with each other. They had about twenty minutes to go before the wedding would start. Robert refused to talk much for fear of throwing up. He played it off as if he was just tired from the night before. *That* had started a round of teasing about why he might be *so* tired. He'd ignored them mostly, but they were only adding to his agitation. Standing he started to pace.

"You alright there son? If you're getting nervous it's pretty natural." Reginald smiled at him from across the room but Robert didn't smile back. This exchange caught the attention of the others in the group and his cousins all walked over to him.

"Robert, you okay? Why don't you sit down and I'll get you some water." Thomas commented, trying to get him to sit.

Robert shook him off and kept moving. His nerves were so worked up that he actually had a light sheen of sweat on his skin.

Cam stepped in front of him stopping his movements. Placing both hands on Robert's shoulders, looking him dead in the eyes. "What do you need me to do?"

Robert finally focused, his mind settling just long enough to respond. "Get everyone out."

Cam didn't hesitate turning to the room and announcing, "Everyone out. Give us some space."

"Aww hell, I knew he was going to fuck it up!"

"Shut up Darrell!" About five voices responded, while Edward pushed his brother out of the tents entrance as everyone exited.

When everyone was gone, Cam focused on the groom. "What's going on?"

Robert loosened his tie. It felt like he was choking. "Man, what the hell did I think I was doing? I'm not husband material."

"Whoa, easy now. Where is this coming from?" Cam was honestly confused. Up until now Robert has been steady as a rock. He'd never gotten upset or annoyed with all the wedding planning, like any sane man would. He'd been more than fine through all of last night, only getting pensive a little over an hour ago.

"I know you love her." Cam stated, coming out of his musing.

"I do and that's the problem. I'm not good enough for her. She'll realize it down the road, then it will be hell on us both."

Cam quietly chuckled. "Look this has to be nerves, you talking crazy. I meant what I said last night. You are the best man I know. I'm proud to call you my friend, my brother. Mika will be proud to call you her husband. She loves you."

"*Love,*" Robert said the word on a sad sneer, before turning his back. "Cam, sometimes love is not enough."

"He's right on that one," Johanna confirmed, walking in.

Cam turned relieved to see her. If anyone could get through to Robert it was his mother. He gave her a thankful smile as she patted his arm.

"Why don't you go on outside with the others Cam. That lovely wedding planner came to get me, since I'm walking in with Robert and we're almost ready to start."

Cam nodded in understanding and left.

Johanna waited silently, giving her son a little more time to organize what he was feeling in his head. He had always been a deep and thoughtful child, and that had carried over into his manhood. When she thought the time was right she spoke. "Talk to me."

The desolate look on his face when he turned broke her heart.

"Mama, I made a mistake. It's not going to work so we might as well end it here."

"Hmm. Is it because of what you said...you don't think love is enough?"

"It wasn't for you and the man who donated his sperm to make me," Robert said resentfully.

Johanna snorted. "No son, it wasn't. But that's because only *I* was in love. It takes two hearts to be fully committed to make a marriage work. You love Mika *and* she loves you. Your relationship will be nothing like your father's and mine. Heck, it's already on a better foundation than mine was."

"I have him in me. What if down the road when she really needs me I let her down? I don't ever want to see the hurt and sadness in her eyes that I saw in yours growing up."

Johanna took his face in her hands. "Robert Lorde, now you listen to me. Have I ever lied to you, even when things were rough or downright bad?"

He shook his head no.

"So believe me when I tell you, you are *nothing* like your daddy. The only thing you have in common with him is your handsome face. It's what I fell for. I thought inside he had what it took to be a good husband and father...but he didn't. But *you* Robert...you have what matters inside."

She poked at his chest. "You have a good heart, a strong backbone, and a nimble mind. You are lucky enough to be blessed with a woman who loves you back, waiting for you to take her hand in marriage. I'm saying this as your mother who knows *all* your faults *and* your strengths. You are an *exceptional* man, and you *will* make an *outstanding* husband and *excellent* father when it's time."

Robert closed his eyes absorbing his mother's words. She never lied to him. He felt something shift and settle in his mind. He would be okay.

"So," Johanna asked. "What are you going to do? It's decision time. Are you getting married to the woman you love today or not?"

"Yeah, I'm getting married. Thank you Mama, for talking some sense into me."

"No thanks needed, I just told the truth. Now, let's get you fixed up." She readjusted his tie and smoothed down his shirt. "Use those baby wipes on that table and wipe that sheen off you. Then come on outside. I'm ready to get my daughter-in-law!"

He watched his mother leave before following her instructions. He loved that woman dearly, as dearly as he loved the amazing woman waiting for him in the other tent. He wouldn't let last-minute, irrational fears make him lose the best thing to ever come into his life.

* * *

The wedding started on time at 5:00 pm, with Robert and his mother entering first. Robert kissed her cheek seating her before taking his own place. Next came the wedding party procession who came to a stop on either side of him. The kids came next. They had decided that his niece would hold the ring bearer's hand and walk down with him. Then the music changed and Mika was framed by both her father and mother walking her to the groom. At first Beverly had balked at the idea, but Robert had seen that she was secretly pleased *and* honored at being included in this way. These were passing thoughts as his eyes locked onto Mika.

To his eyes she was stunning. She held his stare sure and steady as she walked proudly towards him. He saw no hesitation only happiness, a little mischief and a dose of challenge directed his way. Looking at her now it was hard to imagine how he had almost let *anything*—even his own internal demons—keep him from her. He answered her challenge with a smile of his own, full of promise for what the future held for them both.

Mika bit her lip, pretending to listen to the officiant but she couldn't stop looking at Robert. This magnificent man standing next to her was all hers! She never should have agreed to the traditional wedding language. She just wanted the end part where they said "I do". After what seemed like an eternity it was finally time for the vows. Robert and Mika turned to each other clasping hands, as Robert went first.

"Mika 'Trouble" Harrison, I didn't see you coming. Though you had my complete attention as I walked behind you into that restaurant." He ran his eyes up and down her body, and the crowd twittered at the innuendo. "Your energy, your light, grabbed ahold of me and wouldn't let go. You challenged *every* assumption I had about you, and what I wanted in a woman, what *I* wanted out of life. Hell you just challenged me period by being *you*. I realized how much fuller my life could be with you in it. I'm blessed that you are going from being my Princess to my Queen. The best investment I ever made was investing in our love. I love you. All that I have is yours. I can't wait for you to be my rival in sports, the mother of my children, and the love of my life forever."

Mika leaned forward ignoring protocol and gave Robert a sweet, gentle kiss on the lips, then a smile full of love before she begin her own testimony.

"The second I saw you across the aisle on that plane I *knew* you were *not* my type. Later I found you to be arrogant, a stalker, frugal, and high-handed yet also loyal and so kind. Giving in ways that were more important than money could ever be to me. The fact that you're a secret romantic was the cherry on top. You pushed me to confront that I needed companionship, stability, and real love in my life. You made me take the risk of a lifetime by opening my heart to you. You saw me for who I was, and wanted me just as I am. God laughs when it comes to what we think we *want*, then gives us what we actually *need*. He gave me *you*. A strong man to handle a strong woman. To support me, lift me up and take care of me when I don't even know I need it. I plan to do the same for you. I love you Robert Lorde, just the way you are. You *are* just the type of man I need as my *husband,* and I look forward to driving you crazy for the rest of our lives."

Epilogue

There Tamara was full circle back to thinking of her job, which in turn made her glance over at the wedding taking place. Giving up on reading she packed her bag and made her way over to the white tent. There was a line roping off the side and around the back, but nothing to really stop her from coming into the space. The fancy tent had decorative side windows and she could see all the people happily listening to what was being said. Making her way to the back she ducked under the rope, then slipped between the open flaps while all eyes were upfront. The couple were gazing into each other's eyes, so she stood and quietly watched.

The wedding was certainly colorful and full of flowers that was for sure. From the wedding party and guests to the couple tying the knot, color and life abounded. The bride looked beautiful! Face beaming with love and joy as she looked up at the very handsome, dark-skinned brother who was looking down into her eyes.

Even with the job Tamara had she was still a sucker for love and weddings. Something about the pure joy of the moment kept a little kernel of hope alive in her heart. She listened to the couple's vows and admitted that her eyes got a little watery. Although she didn't know the couple she laughed along with the crowd at their heartfelt, funny and uplifting words. The bride went last, and Tamara listened as she recited a list of the groom's faults and assets, all with the biggest smile on her face. Tamara relaxed, this marriage might be one of the lucky ones to make it.

Here was a woman going into a marriage with no blinders on. No fairytale visions of what her mate was supposed to be. Instead, she saw him clearly for who he was. Accepted his faults and praised his good points, and loved him for both. Yeah, they just might make it. Strangely she really hoped they did. Their energy and vibe were infusing her with happiness. Guess her heart wasn't completely dead after all.

She heard a sound to her left, turning her head to see a man standing on the other side of the tent. He seemed relaxed, like he had been there for a while. How had she not noticed him? He was a *fine* man of medium complexion, dressed in a lightweight grey and white t-shirt with an open white shirt over it. He had on white linen pants and what looked to be leather sandals. He had a full beard, though it was cut low along his jawline. More importantly than all that, he was looking right at her.

A slow smile spread across his face, his generous lips stretching wide, showing off ridiculously straight and white teeth. Tamara caught her breath, then lost it again as he brought one finger up to his lips in the universal sign of "shhh, don't say anything". His gesture surprised a smile out of her and she responded by zipping and locking her lips, which only made the stranger across from her smile harder. They were jarred out of their game by the claps and cries of "congratulations" up front. Apparently they had both missed the end of the wedding. As she joined the rest of the crowd in clapping, fine guy to the side made his way over.

"It's good to see I wasn't the only wedding crasher here today."

His voice was warm and playful and he stood at least five inches over her 5'6" frame.

"I plead the fifth on any allegations of being a wedding crasher," Tamara responded in kind.

He gave an easy shrug, stepping slightly closer as the noise in the tent continued to rise in jubilation. "Well I've already told on myself, so I can't take it back." He held out his hand. "I'm Ben Thompson, first time wedding crasher. You?"

She hesitated just a moment before taking his hand. It was big, a little rough, and almost swallowed hers completely. "Tamara Reed...nice to meet you."

If you would like a book club guide for *Not My Type* go to:

http://www.TaylorMadeDaydreams.com/

Thank you for supporting African-American Independent Authors. *If* **you enjoyed the book, please consider leaving a REVIEW on the platform you bought the book from or on Goodreads. Reviews are an easy way you can help any author and in particular Indies get noticed. Reviews can be a one-liner or in depth overview of your thoughts (no spoilers please) or even just a positive "star" rating.**

Join Us For A New Series

"Vacation Love Series"
Winter 2019

Crashing In On Love

After crashing a wedding in Jamaica can two strangers find love?

Tamara Reed spends her days seeing the worst that love has to offer as a divorce lawyer. Yet she still finds herself drawn to weddings, and a secret part of her heart still believes in love. Crashing a wedding while on a much needed vacation finds her meeting a tempting man. He not only catches her attention but sets her blood on fire! After an intense night with him, she sneaks home to forget her vacation fling. That's easier said than done as memories keep her up at night, and her vacation boo tracks her down. Is she ready to take a chance on love?

Benjamin Thompson went on vacation for a little work and a lot of relaxation. Who knew when he took a detour to watch a random wedding, he'd get a chance to "play" as well? The woman he meets takes his breath away and knocks his socks off in the sheets! Barely exchanging any info before having the wildest sex of his life, he wakes up to find his sexy siren gone. Hooked after one taste, he tracks Tamara down only to find that she wants to keep their passionate night a one-time deal. As a successful Realtor and Property Investor he's accustomed to tough negotiations. But he's determined to close this deal no matter what it takes.

By Taylor Love

Join Us For The Final Book

"Instant Chemistry Series"
Spring 2019

One Click For Love

Will a spur of the moment decision to update her dating profile change her life forever?

Brihanna Lorde's female relatives consider her "un-girly". The truth is she's a modern day woman just trying to live her life. With her brother in newly wedded bliss, her family ups the pressure for her to "catch a man". Which is easier said than done for a semi-loner who is a video game programmer. Her quirky and independent personality seems to rub men the wrong way. However, she can admit to wanting a real relationship of her own. Taking a chance on a new online "match" might net her a guy who doesn't scare so easily. Exposing her to desires she didn't even know she had!

Lawrence Townsend is a laid-back unassuming guy, on the brink of turning thirty. While not looking for love exactly, he's definitely ready for more than the "hit it and quit it" hook-ups that define the modern dating scene. As an IT Manager his job is constantly hectic and unpredictable. It's no wonder he likes to take control in the bedroom. The sexy profile of a woman with a twinkle of mischief in her eyes intrigues him, while her prickly exterior heats not only his temper but his passions as well. He's up for the challenge of bending her to his will. But it's a battle that may bruise both their hearts.

By Taylor Love

About the Author

Taylor Love is a new author who calls Michigan her home. Her goal is to write Sexy- Modern-Romance books, featuring African-American couples. Showing that *they* too can have positive and romantic love stories! An avid reader since she was a young girl, she gained a love of writing as well. She loves to read a variety of genres and hopes over time to expand her writing among several of them. She is a lover of learning a "little bit" about many things. She hopes her imagination brings her readers a few hours of enjoyment!

Books by Taylor Love

Running Into You
Not My Type

Stay In Touch!

FACEBOOK
https://www.facebook.com/TaylorMadeDayDreams/

NEWSLETTER (NO SPAM, 2 A MONTH TOPS)
http://eepurl.com/duB-Fn

TWITTER
https://twitter.com/TaylorLoveWrite

INSTAGRAM
https://www.instagram.com/taylorlovewriter/

BOOKBUB
https://www.bookbub.com/profile/taylor-love?list=author_books

BLOG
http://taylormadedaydreams.com/blog.html

10378167R00142

Made in the USA
Lexington, KY
26 September 2018